SANDY

CAUGHT
BY AN
EX-CON

A TRUE STORY
OF
DIVINE INTERVENTION

Caught by an Ex-con
by Sandy Whalen

ISBN: 978-1-935018-96-4

Interior Design: Leo Ward
Cover Design: Randy Johnson

PUBLISHED BY:
Five Stones Publishing
A DIVISION OF:
The International Localization Network
randyjohnson@ilncenter.com

This book is dedicated first and foremost to my precious Lord and Savior, Jesus Christ who gave me a reason to live when I didn't think I could go on another day and gave me eternal life now and forever!

I also want to dedicate this to my dear late husband and soul mate Patrick who filled my life with more love and joy than my heart could have ever imagined.

Also, to my family and many friends who prayed and stood with me through the triumphs and heartbreaks for many years.

Finally, to those who have ever been incarcerated or are now. I pray this book gives you hope and joy in the midst of your trials.

To all of you this book is dedicated. It is our story together and I thank you from the bottom of my heart.

With much love,

Sandy Whalen

8-13-15

Dearest Gail!

It's finally finished!

Thanks for being part of my story! You ain't seen nothin' yet! God has great plans for you! Is. 43:18-19

Love Sandy

Contents

Well, this is finally the time. Years later. Only God knows how many times I have started this book- four or five - something like that. Each time I tried, my tears hit the pages of my pad faster than my ink. Sometimes I would curl up in a ball on my living room floor and cry like there was no tomorrow. I told God, "I can't do this. I just can't!" Then, I'd stop for a while only later to end up with the same unfortunate results. Now maybe, just maybe, this is the time...

I remember my dreams as a little girl - don't all little girls play princess? I know I sure did! Our knight in shining armor will come riding on a white horse and literally sweep us off our feet. He will catch us away to live with him forever in the glistening beautiful castle just over the rollling hills in a far away country. We will never suffer sorrow or pain again but only joy, happiness and perfect love. And we can't wait for that day. I guess I, for one, thought it might just happen on this earth.

Let's face it. Life isn't easy; in fact, most of the time life is pretty difficult. However when we experience hard times knowing that a loving God is always with us cheering us on, we can go through any crisis with hope. My life has not been an easy road, as you will read, yet I would never trade it for anone else's. God gave me this one life to live to the fullest.

As you read my story of crime, prison, world escapades, love and loss, my prayer is that you will be challenged and encouraged in your own life. God gave you *your* life to live to the very fullest also - no matter *what* comes your way. I dare you to start today even as you read my amazing adventure.

My late husband. Ooh, that stings. Yes, in many ways that's exactly what he was - late, at least in my limited estimation. I had experienced a traumatic divorce that ended fourteen years of marriage nineteen years earlier. This left me raising two sons, ages ten and thirteen, all alone. For years after my divorce I prayed for my knight in shining armor to come galloping into my life. I wondered, did the man of my dreams really exist, or was this person only to be found in fairy tales?

As I prayed for my future soul mate, I wrote a detailed list specifying what I wanted in a man and I prayerfully presented my list to God. I knew that only through the grace of God could I possibly ever meet this man that I so deeply desired.

Even though I believed that this could happen, I knew that it would probably be far off into the future. After all, I was already fifty-two years old and realized that the prospects of finding the gem of a man that I had in mind were slim to none; time was certainly not on my side.

Trying to find the man of my dreams in the usual worldly way surely wasn't working for me and I tried everything. The bar scene and party life soon became boring and extremely depressing; there had to be more than this, I thought. Eventually, I stopped all of that craziness and became involved in a few Christian single groups. However I still found myself looking for 'Mr. Right' behind every door, volleyball net, Denny's Restaurant, Bible study group and single's function - and still - no husband.

I finally thought, Lord God, either You do this for me or it isn't going to happen! I actually quit dating altogether for many years and ended up trading the empty dating lifestyle for a life filled with great joy and satisfaction in serving God's children by loving the poor and the unlovable.

So here I was, 19 years later. I stood in the misson's kitchen, the Rochester Urban Center that I directed with my co-worker Joanne. (We served approximately 10,000 meals per year through our soup kitchen, coffeehouse and other programs.)

We were getting ready to serve the Wednesday lunch to about 30 homeless and very needy folks. There was a knock at the back door; I hoped it might be a new volunteer which we were always in need of. I answered the door and a handsome, though definitely disheveled gentleman poked his head through the doorway and said, "I'm here to help. Could you use an extra hand today?"

I said, "Sure, come on in. We can use you in the kitchen."

He wasn't too excited about that; I soon discovered that he could hardly boil water!

"I really have a heart for the brokenhearted and would love to hang out here and minister to them," he said. "That's great," I said, "but we really need help in the kitchen, so you can do both. What did you say your name was?"

"Patrick, Patrick Whalen," he replied.

"Sounds good, Patrick; now, let's get to work."

And, to work we went!

Patrick truly did have a deep compassion for the lost, the broken and the homeless. Prior to coming to the Urban Center, he had been spending his time visiting several missions and shelters and sharing God's love, telling them about Jesus. That is how he found out about our work at the Urban Center.

Pat would busy himself daily making peanut butter and jelly sandwiches at home, then take the bus downtown to pass them out to the hungry and homeless. He also was very active through his church visiting people who were in various stages of need. He would give them bags of groceries and tell them about the unconditional love of his Savior, Jesus.

As I said, we were always in need of help at the Center...

Friday nights we hosted a large coffeehouse with Christian bands, free food, coffee and prayer.

Saturday evenings 60 to 100 people came for a large soup kitchen and service.

Wednesdays and Thursdays were meals with Bible studies.

There were also jail visits one to two times per week as well as picking up the food, organizing, preaching, praying, and more. We were all very busy.

Funny, I thought, Patrick said he was going to volunteer at the Center one day per week; now here he was - at least five days per week helping in any way he could. Hmm... I was amazed to see how easily we flowed together. We prayed together often for our homeless and struggling friends who asked for prayer. What a blessing it was to hear how our prayers just melded together, hand in glove. As we worked, laughed, shared and prayed together, our friendship naturally grew. My heart was starting to be touched by his and vice versa. I must admit that I was starting to get a little nervous!

Two months after we met, Pat, myself and six volunteers from the Center flew to the LA Dream Center for a one-week mission trip. The LA Dream Center is a Christian mission outreach in Los Angeles, California. That was the experience of a lifetime. We were working with hundreds of homeless people on skid row. We fed them, prayed with them, ministered to prostitutes and helped so many people in need. All of us were full of God's joy and were so blessed to see how the LA Dream Center was reaching literally thousands of poor and needy people and helping transform their lives.

It seemed every time I turned around, Pat was right behind me. We had a blast; I thought it was great to have a nice male friend!

Our seats on the plane just happened to be next to each other for the eight-hour trip home to Rochester, NY. I was reading a magazine on the flight, when Pat blurted out to me, "I'm looking for a relationship."

I squirmed in my seat and thought, what is he talking about? It sounds like he's asking me to get involved with him! He must be out of his mind! However, I nonchalantly replied, "That's really nice, Pat. I'm sure God will send you a wonderful wife someday."

Yes, he was cute, but he was just a friend to me. I had been hurt so many times and had experienced too many false alarms. I had heard enough come-on lines from guys to last a lifetime, so I was more than a little cautious; I really wasn't interested in hearing any more!

Right after that trip, our feelings for each other began to escalate. We called each other almost daily and talked for hours on end about ministry. We kept it all business, but after I hung up the phone one day, I thought, *he is so much fun to talk with. I could talk to him forever! Could he possibly be the one that I have been waiting for all these years? No,* I shook my head and thought, *don't be foolish, don't even think that way!*

About two months after we met, I began getting very strong signals from Pat that he was more than just a little interested in me. I was feeling very attracted to him as well. I knew that it was time we had a serious talk to discuss our relationship and to set some ground rules in place.

It was decided that we would go to an out-of-the-way restaurant where no one would recognize us. After all, people do talk and I didn't want anyone to think that we were dating, because we certainly weren't. Well, the adage held true that states: 'the best laid plans of mice and men often go astray'. The waitress that took our order turned out to be one of the regular visitors from the Urban Center; so much for keeping things quiet!

Before our actual meeting, I thought through what I wanted to come out of our discussion. I was not going to say that I was attracted to him, in fact I had planned to say just the opposite. I had decided to tell him that although I thought he might be interested in me, there were some things in his past that bothered me. Especially troublesome to me was another relationship that was still unsettled and up in the air; there was no way I would ever consider dating him with that unresolved issue. And that is exactly what I told him.

Even after that meeting, Pat was relentless in asking me out. Here's what I wrote in my journal a few days after that conversation:

Pat asked me out again tonight; it was his birthday. I said that I can't go out with him if things are still unresolved with that old relationship…yet I am VERY attracted to him. O Lord, it's been so long! Pat put his arm around my waist as I played the piano tonight at the Center. I told him to put it down as it made me nervous. Yet, I didn't want to tell him that at all. O Lord, help me! I do get lonely. I really like him. I must be crazy, Lord. I guess I'm just lonely.

Pat still continued wildly pursuing me. One night while we were serving the homeless, he asked me if I would like to go to the circus with him. I'm not sure what came over me, but I answered, "Sure, but I really don't like the circus. Can we go somewhere else?"

He suggested indoor miniature golf in a mall quite a distance from the city. This sounded good to me ... not a chance of seeing someone from the Center there! I told him this was a friendship date and that my 'adopted' daughter, Liz, would be coming along. He said that was fine with him.

My 'adopted' daughter was a precious sixteen-year-old homeless young lady that I had taken in one month earlier. She had run away from various group homes and was living with some pretty rough gangs on the street. She was so helpless and innocent the night I met her at the Center and was literally shaking with fear at the thought of facing another night sleeping on the damp cold sidewalks a few blocks away. I took her in that night and she lived with me for the next seven months. God touched Liz mightily and she decided to follow Jesus and not the gangs after that.

So we three, Pat, Liz and I went to the mall and no sooner had we entered when we were met by Renee, another volunteer from the Center! Oh great, I thought, she's going to tell everyone at the Center that Pat and I are dating! Pat proceeded to take Renee off to the side for a few minutes. Long after we were married, he told me what he had said to her... "Renee, God told me that Sandy is going to be my wife and we are going to get married before too long. Please pray for us." Renee thought that was wonderful and would pray for us.

Looking back, I am so glad that I had no idea beforehand that this was happening or I would have run as far and as fast as I could from this crazy guy; no way I was going to get caught by this handsome ex-con!

Soon after, Pat and I both went on separate retreats and sought to hear from God about this budding romance. On my retreat, I had taken a book along that I thought was about knowing God more. Well, it turned out that it was mostly about finding a husband. If I believed that someone was clearly placed in my life, just maybe that someone was the man that God had sent to me in answer to my prayers ... and if so, I should not be afraid. The author said that maybe I should go for it! Imagine, every word in that book spoke to me directly about Patrick. I was so overwhelmed that I wrote a poem expressing my feelings on the retreat:

O Lord, It's been a long time, a long time I've been alone.
Lord you have been with me, always soothing my fears, always catching my tears.
Lord, you've been so faithful to me each and every day,
I know you answer prayer
In your time and in your way.
So now I lay before you the matters of my heart; the things that I have prayed for, the things that I desire.
Lord I give you every part of my heart and soul.
I know that you are faithful. You'll guide me; you'll never let me go.

On the night of our reunion after our retreats, Pat was so excited that he seemed ready to jump out of the seat of the car as we were driving home from a church service. He told me about a prophetic word that was given to him at his retreat. He said that the prophecy was about me! I wondered what in the world was coming. Pat bellowed out as I drove the car,

"The word spoken over me was, 'There is a woman praying for you. That woman is your WIFE – I know you're not married but she is your future wife!'"

I said, "Stop it, stop it! I'm driving the car ... I'll have a wreck!" I started laughing and crying, then laughing and crying all over again! I was still trying to drive the car. This was too much. Oh God, I thought, Could this really be? After nineteen long years?

Before I go any further into our relationship, there are a few things you should know about Patrick. I'll begin with the list that I had submitted to God in prayer regarding my future husband. It went like this:

- A man after God's own heart. He would love Jesus first in his life and serve Him with his whole heart.
- He would be handsome—dashing, in fact!
- He would love me unconditionally, just the way I was.
- He would have the same heart as me to reach the lost, the hurting and homeless for Jesus.
- He would have a great sense of humor and make me laugh.
- We could communicate well and minister together as one.
- He would love and accept my family and children.
- He would be kindhearted and compassionate to all.
- He would be an ex-convict with an exciting story!

Yes, that's right. I prayed that God would actually send me an ex-convict. Now before you think I am totally crazy, let me explain why ...

Years earlier I had attended a church that had from time to time brought in a few ex-cons to share their stories. They would talk about their experiences with guns, drugs, jail, being shot at, and so on. Yet, they displayed God's joy and peace because they had found salvation through the redeeming power of Jesus Christ. Every time I heard one of their accounts, I just sat on the edge of my seat spellbound. One night I prayed, *Lord, if it is Your will that I get remarried, please let it be to an ex-con with that kind of testimony. May it be so powerful that it will be life changing to all who hear it.*

I'll never forget when I first heard about Pat's past life; we were in a Social Security office helping a friend from the Urban Center get on disability. We were in a group talking when I overheard Pat saying something about robbing drug stores and then overdosing on half of the drugs that he had stolen! My eyes bulged out! "Did you have a gun when you did this?" I asked. He replied, "Yes, of course I did!" Whew- I quickly took two steps backward. *This is too much*, I thought, *what if Pat is still like that?*

Bit by bit, I heard stories of Pat's very dark and sordid past of drugs and crime… Pat began using alcohol when he was twelve years old. He would sneak out of his parents' home, get drunk and return home later only to proceed to vomit all over his bed. Pat began to develop this sneaky nature at a very young age. A good example is how he handled not going to church on Sundays, which was the last thing he wanted to do. A few minutes before the family was ready to leave for church, Pat would sneak into the family car and pump the gas pedal, flooding the engine. Soon, his entire family would hop into the car prepared to go to church only to find out that for *some strange reason* they couldn't get the car started. The only ones in the family who were disappointed were Mom and Dad!

In addition to the alcohol Pat was using and the devious streak he was developing, he began stealing cases of beer--and anything else that wasn't nailed down. Pat had built up an intense anger, especially against his father. He felt that no one really cared about him and he wasn't able to receive love from his family even though they did deeply love him. His rebellion continued to increase.

He ran away from home and quit high school to embarrass his father. Soon he began regularly tripping on LSD. He joined the Marine Corps, but continued using drugs even when he was in the military, in fact, his drug use increased to the point where he began shooting-up heroin. When his drug use was finally discovered, he was arrested and imprisoned for ninety days. Though Pat could have received a dishonorable discharge, he was instead granted a general discharge, which held no charge against him. However, he left the military with an even deeper drug habit and more pent-up anger in his heart.

Pat then teamed up with a woman and together they started drug trafficking to and from New York City. They had found a methamphetamine connection in Canada that was only three people down from the chemist who made it. Being that close to the source, they were pretty confident that it was good stuff. They began smuggling crystal meth across the Canadian border and things were going pretty well until they were arrested.

Their case was later dismissed and Pat was never charged with any crime! They learned later that the man who was on the second tier from the chemist was thrown off a 16-story building in Canada! In retrospect, I can see God's hand was on him through all that; Pat and his girlfriend had been messing with an extremely deadly crew! A short time later, Pat was arrested for possession of 16 bags of heroin and received his first prison bid of one year. *(A bid is prison slang for prison sentence).*

The drugs were almost as plentiful in jail as out; when Pat was released, he was more addicted to drugs than ever before. His life was drugs, drugs, and more drugs. He and a new woman partner soon had to have more money to support their overwhelming drug habit and they were looking for some quick cash. Breaking into drug stores seemed to be the perfect solution. In short order, Pat and his partner burglarized several drug stores in only one week and were arrested with over $100,000 worth of drugs!

They had also gone on a crime spree of robbing 'Stop N Go' stores. Pat said that he would smash the front window of the stores with a large sledgehammer, then run directly to the safe. It usually had a front door on it that bulged out, according to the design. Pat knew that the safe was spring loaded. Pat would flex his muscles and swing the sledgehammer with all his strength right onto the center of the door. Voila! The door would spring open, just like a 'jack-in-the-box' and there would lay all the cash for the taking! With all their newfound money, Pat and his partner were able to purchase more drugs, which only clouded their minds and hardened their consciences more than ever.

Captured again, Pat stood in front of the judge, awaiting his sentencing. This time, he received two years to life in prison. Pat was in shock. He was ordered to one of the highest security prisons in the country, the infamous Attica State Prison in Attica, NY where 39 people had lost their lives during prison riots in 1971. The future undoubtedly did not look very bright for Patrick.

Fear gripped Pat's heart as he entered prison, especially when he learned that a nearby mental institution had recently closed and many men who were criminally insane ended up in the Attica prison- along with him.

Pat was assigned to work in the mess hall where he quickly found a way to steal fruit juice and sugar on a regular basis. The bakery was located next to the mess hall and he was able to swipe baker's yeast. Before long, Pat was making wine. He kept his winery hidden in his cell behind his bed. He was making eight gallons of wine every eight days in prison! To me, this was unbelievable. Remember, this was Attica prison. Besides staying drunk on the wine he was making, Pat was able to trade gallons of wine for a couple of joints (marijuana) or anything else available.

God's mighty hand on Patrick's life was evident over and over again. One day while he was in Attica, Pat's stomach began giving him incredible pain. The doctor could not find out what the problem was. His stomach had bloated and was very protruded, so Pat was rushed to the emergency room. As it turned out, Pat had consumed wine that had not fully fermented yet and it was still turning into alcohol inside of his stomach!

One reason that Pat tried to keep drunk continually was to enable him to cope with all the violence he was surrounded by in prison. Almost every day in the summer, someone would get stabbed in the yard. Retaliation and gang fights were common place. Everyone carried some sort of a knife or, as the inmates called it, a shank.

There were three horrific attacks that Pat experienced first hand. The first attack that Pat saw involved three men being stabbed in the mess hall. Their blood was splattered everywhere. Panic ensued and the guards rushed into the mess hall with tear gas. Pat recalled that time as a living hell—being trapped in a room filled with tear gas and no way to escape.

Two weeks after that incident, while Pat was serving in the food line, a woman guard was brutally slashed across her face with a razor blade. The entire attack only took three seconds and scarred the young lady for the rest of her life.

The third episode was when a female civilian employee was raped and murdered in the walk-in cooler. Just the previous day, she had written up Pat for disciplinary action, thus Pat became a prime suspect. Attica was in lock-down for days—everyone locked in their cells; all privileges ceased. Finally the murderer was discovered and charged with the crime. Thankfully, Pat was cleared of any involvement with the incident.

One would think that by living a lifestyle of crime, drugs and incarceration, Pat would have wanted to change and do whatever it took to be free from the demons that bound him. However, this was only the beginning of his rebellion against himself, society and ... God. Patrick's life was about to dip even deeper into corruption and criminal behavior. Through it all, God's love never stopped drawing Pat. God never gave up on him and yet, Pat slid down even deeper and deeper.

After one year in Attica prison, Pat applied for a transfer to a prison closer to home in hopes that his family would visit him from time to time. He was allowed to transfer to a medium security prison somewhat closer to his family. Shortly after his arrival, being bored and lonely, Pat teamed up with two other inmates and planned a great escape. They thought they had the perfect plan.

They arranged for a car to be waiting outside the prison fence. They made sure that the trunk was stashed with weapons as they would need them for their next heist. However, the escape was foiled when Pat's two buddies got tangled up on top of the barbed wire fence! Pat got stuck underneath the fence but somehow was able to wiggle his way out and run back into his cell without ever getting caught. Though Patrick was spotted, the guards could not positively identify him and he was never charged with an escape attempt.

In time with the help of a counselor, Pat became more stable in prison. He was even elected in a landslide election to be the inmate grievance representative. After three years time, he was released from prison with life parole.

Pat wanted to settle down and try to live a normal life. He married a woman friend who had started visiting him in jail and had high hopes for the future. He was able to get a job at a convenience store and eventually became the manager. Things were looking up but the desire for drugs soon pulled Pat away from the regular life he was living. Before long, Pat began forging prescriptions for drugs. He got as many drugs as he could handle, but when it comes to drugs, enough is never enough.

Pat's cravings for a higher high only increased. He found a new crime partner, Sue. Soon they decided to burglarize a local drugstore for more drugs. They were stoned on cocaine as they approached the rear of the store. Pat threw a rope with a large hook on the end, on top of the roof, quickly shimmied up the rope, and helped his new partner up as well. After 45 minutes, Pat was finally able to cut through the roof top. He then pulled out a ceiling tile and saw that they were right over the pharmacy counter. All set, he thought. Sue remained on the roof as a lookout while Pat lowered his ladder down to get their jackpot. When he didn't return in 30 minutes, Sue became nervous. She thought Pat might be overdosing on the drugs right then and there. She thought they were going to just get in and out.

Sue decided to enter the hole in the roof and check on Pat, but lost her footing on the way down. She had tried crawling along the upper beams and crossbars in the ceiling when suddenly her feet slipped. Now all her weight landed on the plaster ceiling and the ceiling gave way; half her body was entangled in the plaster ceiling! Pat heard the loud crash and assumed it was the police. He thought the only way out was to run straight through the front plate glass window. As he was preparing to make his exit, he heard Sue yelling for help from the back of the store.

Pat ran to help her to find that she was stuck in the ceiling with her long legs wiggling through the plaster! After Pat wrangled her down, they ran behind the pharmacy counter and grabbed syringes, filled them up with liquid Demerol and began shooting it into their veins. They continued to get high in the store for almost three hours when they realized there were red flashing lights all around the outside of the store. Definitely time to get out of there fast, but there wasn't any way they could, so they quickly ducked low behind the counter.

An officer started rattling and shaking the back door. It looked like they were hopelessly trapped. Sue begged Pat to surrender, but Pat was determined to escape. No police had entered the store yet, though it was totally surrounded by then. The only way out was up, Pat thought.

They made a dash to the back of the store where the ladder was still stuck in the ceiling. He scurried up the ladder with two large bags of drugs. Once on the roof, he could see six police cruisers out front. He rushed back inside to help Sue escape. Morning was breaking and they knew they would soon be seen on top of the building. Though Pat never prayed, he thought if he was ever going to pray, now was the time! With all his strength, he cried out to God, "Lord, if you get me out of this, I promise I'll quit and never do this again!" Suddenly without warning, the patrol cars turned off their lights and one by one left the scene. Pat and Sue ran to the back of the roof and saw a huge dumpster below which they both jumped into and managed to make a safe getaway to Sue's car up the street!

Pat and Sue returned to Sue's house and immediately began to celebrate their big score. They stayed up for three days getting high on all the drugs. They could barely function as they were close to a blackout state. Pat finally left Sue's house with his bag of drugs and checked into a local hotel.

Pat didn't realize what reality was any more as he now was having both sight and sound hallucinations. Pat proceeded to the bathroom to shoot up and thought he heard two policemen in the hallway. Since he had a lot of cocaine on him, he decided he'd better use it all before the cops caught him. Delusional, Pat shot himself up with a suicidal fix. As he stood up to leave the bathroom, his body collapsed as he went into a grand mal seizure.

When he finally woke up, Pat was paralyzed on his entire left side. When he tried to walk, his left leg dragged across the carpet. As the seizure subsided, Pat still crazed with cocaine, scooped up the remaining spilled cocaine off the floor with his one working hand, loaded it into a syringe and gave himself yet another hit. Death was knocking on his door as he passed out. Funny thing, the police never were in the hallway. It was another hallucination. Amazingly, all the effects of the seizure disappeared.

Pat's life continued spiraling downward. He forgot about his promise to God although his wife remained by his side through all of this. Pat was admitted to various detox and rehab centers; yet every time he was released, he and his wife would celebrate with a fresh bottle of champagne. The addiction was only hiding for the time being, but never gone.

Pat seemed incorrigible. Soon Pat ran into his old friend, Joe; they had forged prescriptions together a few years back. They decided to get some drugs and do life the way Pat knew best. Time to burglarize another drugstore.

Soon, they were on the roof of a drugstore for their next caper. Pat and Joe attempted to saw off a large metal grate to enter. Joe had previously been in a terrible accident and had a prosthetic right arm with a hook for a hand, but the work on the roof went well in spite of his handicap. However, when they broke the last weld, the grate flipped sideways and Joe's artificial hook got caught in the grate as it plummeted downward. The grate landed squarely on the counter below with Joe's prosthetic arm attached! No matter, getting the drugs was all that mattered now.

In seconds, they were at the pharmacy counter stuffing their bags with drugs, filling needles with Demerol and getting high, as well as trying to reattach Joe's artificial arm. Pat had pretty much given up on a normal life at this point, but one thing he knew— do not get caught, no matter what, but it was soon too late for that. Police rushed the store and in seconds, Pat felt the cold metal barrel of a revolver pressing into his eardrum. Pat and Joe had no choice but to surrender this time. For some odd reason, the police handcuffed Pat and Joe together along with one of the full bags of drugs and the police put them into the back of their police car and left them alone.

Being crazed with drugs, Joe was able to pass many Demerol tablets to Pat while they were in the car and they overdosed right in the back seat of the patrol car. Pat vaguely remembered getting interrogated at the police station but he was so close to unconsciousness that they sped him away to the local emergency room. The next thing Pat remembered was waking up in jail two days later. Pat was later convicted and sentenced to two to four years in a minimum security prison. He actually thought that was a very short sentence and he felt pretty smug about that!

Pat was finally growing weary of the criminal lifestyle after being incarcerated yet again. He was now labeled a career criminal. Thoughts of suicide invaded his mind. Could there ever be any hope for him? Pat had lost all his friends and most of his family.

He wondered if there even was a God. Did God exist; much less love him, such a career criminal? Pat knew beyond a shadow of a doubt that he had to find some real answers. Rehabs didn't work. Crime certainly did not pay. There had to be something, or Some One who could change his miserable, broken life. He noticed a very dedicated group of church men that came weekly to hold Bible studies at the prison. It couldn't hurt to attend, he reasoned. They always were so happy and joyful, even if no one came to their study. It looked like they had something that Pat needed desperately.

Pat finally started attending the Bible study regularly and at one point asked Jesus to change his life and become his Lord and Savior. The Bible group was allowed to take many of the inmates, including Pat, to be baptized at a beautiful lake in the Adirondacks in upstate New York, very close to the prison. Pat was doing much better, but he didn't really understand the commitment he had made to God. He had accepted Jesus into his mind, but not completely into his heart, a huge difference. However, during the twenty months Pat spent at the prison, he did no alcohol or drugs, which was a first for him. Pat started to feel great peace and contentment for the first time in his life. During the worship services he could sense the tangible presence of God. He had never been exposed to that before and he knew he needed much more. He had to have a deeper walk with God.

While still in prison, Pat began to walk with a strange gait. Sometimes both his legs would give out and Pat would fall down with no warning. He was taken to a hospital in Rochester, NY, for a diagnosis. After many tests the diagnosis came back: multiple sclerosis. That was devastating news for Pat. Again, God's mighty hand of grace and mercy was on Patrick to spare his life. A few weeks later, Pat woke up and every one of his symptoms was completely gone. The doctors called it a remission. Pat called it a miracle. The disease never returned.

During these years, Pat fathered three beautiful girls. Because of his life of crime and incarceration, Pat saw very little of their growing up years. Pat wrote in his journal later of his torment and sadness as he realized how he had abandoned them as children. He truly asked God to forgive him. In time, Pat told each of them how sorry he was for not being there for them. They still loved their father despite all the pain they had gone through growing up without a father. Eventually, all three relationships were fully restored which became a real joy to Patrick. He thought the world of his daughters. They grew up to be beautiful women, two with children of their own.

After Pat's release from prison, his walk with God was still a little shaky and the enemy of his soul knew where he was weak. Little by little, Pat turned to drugs once again. He entered two more rehab programs and was finally coming to realize that even a thousand hits would never be enough. After his treatment programs, Pat stayed free from drugs and crime for quite a while this time.

He was able to attend college at night and landed a very respectable job as a cost estimator for a large Rochester company. He did so well they promoted him to national sales manager. It looked like the days of being a drug addict and career criminal were behind him. However, the temptations began again when Pat was issued an expense account and company credit card to treat his clients as Pat traveled all over the country on business trips. Before long, cocaine and heroin were again flowing into his veins.

Then came more.... drugs, divorce, fired from job, surgery, diabetes ...

Entering yet another drug rehab program, Pat was diagnosed as an anti-social deviant with no hope of recovery – ever. Before long, his marriage of ten years ended in divorce. He was fired from his job. Not long after, Pat needed major back surgery for two ruptured disks and was diagnosed with diabetes. Though Pat didn't think he could go on any longer, God never forgot him. Pat had given up on God and life and decided to go on one last binge – hoping to end it all for good this time. He woke up from a blackout after giving himself another enormous hit. He was still alive. He would have to face another day. He wondered, will this ever end?

After months of total misery and more drug abuse, Pat cried out to God in total desperation. He was serious this time. He knew he was losing his life, his health and all he knew. He had reached his bottom. With God's mighty intervention and deliverance, AA meetings and new friends supporting him, Pat was able to get totally free from the drugs and addictions in his life. He started attending Bible studies and church and realized he needed to submit his will to God 100%. There was no other way to be and stay free. Pat was filled with God's Holy Spirit and at long last he saw his life change dramatically. Jesus alone had given him the hope he so desperately needed.

Pat's entire personality began to change when God took complete control. Pat's anger, hate, rage, bitterness and fear turned into God's peace, love, kindness, forgiveness and faith. Only a mighty God could take a wreck of a life like Pat's and make him into a gentle and kind human being who truly loved everyone with God's unconditional love. I was about to find out firsthand.

Chapter 6

Was He Really the One?

I slipped my hand into Pat's hand for the very first time; it was our second date. A warm excitement went all through my body as I realized that we were beginning to behave and look like a real couple already. We had just come from a wonderful evening of celebrating the Seder at a Messianic temple, a Jewish ceremonial dinner that commemorates the Exodus. They had run out of kosher food, so they sent out for Chinese - really! We just laughed as our eyes locked thinking about what might lie ahead for us.

Pat had planned a visit to his hometown the next week to visit his family. Due to his loss of peripheral vision, Pat had stopped driving and was going by Greyhound bus. I cheerfully offered to take him to the bus station but before he got out of my car, he handed me a gift. I unwrapped the small box and inside was a beautiful glass angel holding a red heart.

Pat said, "*You're* that angel and you're holding *my* heart."

This is too much!, I thought as I opened the card that came with the gift. My hands were trembling as I read the words he had scribbled in dark letters, "I'm falling in love."

"Oh Patrick!" I gasped.

We just stared into each others' eyes. I couldn't even think straight at that time. I could actually *sense* love in the air.

I sheepishly said, "I feel pretty much the same way."

My heart seemed to be beating out of my chest a thousand times per minute. We grabbed hands, not wanting to ever let go. We prayed for each other and in just a few moments, he was out of the car and onto the bus.

The five days Pat was gone to see his family seemed like an eternity. Finally he came home. The moment he saw me in the crowd at the station, he ran up to me and gave me a big hug and said, "You're right; *abstinence* does make the heart grow fonder!" I giggled and said, "No, Pat, no silly! The word is *'absence'* not *'abstinence'*!"

As we started dating, we discussed our relationship and decided to refer to it as courtship instead of dating. Courtship means entering into a relationship with the intent of going toward marriage. We both knew we were not going to date and have a relationship for the sake of having companionship. We had both seen how devastating that can be. We desired to seek God's will throughout our courtship.

From the beginning, we also made a commitment: first to God; then to one another to remain pure until our wedding day, if that indeed was where God was leading us. Because of many past mistakes in relationships, we both knew we needed guidelines to help us stay pure. I asked Pat to please respect my wishes. We would not even kiss until we were engaged; however we knew that was going to be really be difficult for both of us. By God's grace, we kept that commitment to God and to one another. Day by day, I felt our love grow stronger even though neither of us had said those 'three little words'—yet.

We continued to work and minister together; as time passed we both sensed a genuine flowing together as if we were already one in the spirit. As we prayed with people, our words would just complement one another and I could sense a oneness that I had never felt with anyone before. God continued to draw us closer.

I must say, in my mind as we were courting, I would check off first *this point* and, then *that point*. I realized as time went by that this relationship truly was no mistake. Maybe God was in the middle of this after all!

Many times I asked God to speak to my heart from His Word. Years before, I had started writing down words to me that

I believed were from the Holy Spirit. Later I realized, God had done the exact same thing for Patrick. He had notebooks full of words that God had given him before I had ever met him. Here is one very special 'word' that I wrote down from the Lord in my journal one month after our first date:

Sandy, you've asked Me for surprises and I am truly in the midst of surprising you! Eye has not seen nor ear heard what I have stored up for those that love Me. I have so much to give you. My child, you have only just begun to reap what I have promised you. For you are My treasured possession, My own special handiwork and I have made you for My pleasure. It gives Me much pleasure to give you the desires of your heart. I am not slow but I am always on time. You will see.

Trust Me one day at a time. Do not worry. Don't try to figure everything out. Just know that I love you so much and I choose to give you the things you have asked for – every single one of them. Be patient; I am with you. More and more you will see and I will confirm that indeed I have placed this special man at your side. I know you still are overwhelmed for it will be more than you could ever hope or think or ask. Wait on Me. I will NOT disappoint.

Undoubtedly, the Lord seemed to be pointing me to marrying this man that He had put before me. I was accustomed to going on spiritual retreats two to three times per year and thought I had better get away again and really seek God about all that was going on in my heart.

I needed to know for certain if Pat was the man that I was to marry, so I made another list of things and asked the Lord to answer it as confirmation that Pat was indeed the one I had been waiting for. I offered it to God in prayer. I never told Pat anything about the list. Following are a few of the things on that list:

- Pat would have a worldwide vision to reach millions with the Gospel.
- To dance in worship before the Lord. Most men I know do not!
- For Pat's old relationship to be totally dissolved.

- He would want to get some Bible training to become a minister/pastor.
- He would ask me what my middle name was within three days! He never had asked so I felt like he didn't care about that.
- He would give me a romantic card very soon!
- He would be able to drive *me* all around, not vice versa. I didn't enjoy driving very much and Pat had stopped driving due to vision problems.

Only a few days after I prayed, Pat came to the Urban Center and said, "You know, I don't even know your middle name. What is it?" I was so excited as I simply said, "Carol!"

A couple of days later, Pat presented me with my first romantic card which I held dear to my heart. I knew that God was answering my prayers.

Within one week of praying, he told me that he had an actual vision of millions of lost people with their heads hung down. He knew he was called to preach the Gospel of Jesus Christ to the lost anywhere God would send him.

A short time later, he *accidentally* ended up at a church that he had never attended before. A few days later, Pat attended their men's retreat. During that retreat, God spoke to his heart to get up and praise Him in the dance, so Pat obeyed, his first time ever dancing! One of the first things he said to me after the retreat was, "I have no idea why, but God told me to 'get up and dance' so I did and I want to keep dancing for Him!"

Within two weeks, Pat and I attended a special deliverance service in another city. We had no idea what topics were going to be taught. One of the topics was about old relationships and ungodly soul-ties to another. Ungodly soul-ties are emotional and spiritual ties to another person that are formed through sin entering a relationship and creating attachments that are very hard to be broken- which Pat had to his old girlfriend. By God's Spirit, those ungodly ties were broken off Pat that day and he was completely finished with that relationship forever.

Pat and I had discussed his attending a local Bible school, but he was dead set against it. He had never had any official Bible training and said that he didn't need any and that was that. A few weeks later, I asked him if he would just pray about it anyway. He agreed.

The very next morning, he came to the Center. He didn't even greet me but went immediately to the phone and called Elim Bible Institute in Lima, New York and requested their information packet.

I heard him say, "Yes, I'm interested in your full three-year Bible program."

I almost fainted right then and there! Later, Pat told me that God woke him in the middle of the night and said, *"Go to Bible school!"* God was usually very clear and direct with Patrick. Again, God was truly answering all my prayers.

I think God may have saved the best for last. Since Pat had lost his peripheral vision he didn't feel safe to drive a car any longer. Pat usually took the bus to the Center but I always drove him home. Not long after I compiled my second list, I was driving Pat home after our soup kitchen had closed for the evening. While I was driving and talking to him, I grew increasingly frustrated that he couldn't drive. That meant that I would need to drive him everywhere all the time if we were to be married. The eye doctors had said that there was nothing they could do to repair his eyes.

Enough is enough, I thought. I said, "Patrick, I believe God can heal your eyes and you will be able to drive again. Let's believe for a miracle." Without Pat having really any time to respond, I quickly slapped my right hand over his eyes while I steered the car with the other. "In Jesus' name," I prayed, "eyes be healed and opened up right now. Clear vision be restored. In Jesus' name I call it done! Amen!"

I then lowered my hand and continued driving. That was all I said. Short and sweet. Pat, doubtingly, opened his eyes. Unbelievably, his vision had been completely restored—instantly! Praise God's Holy name! I never had seen anything quite this dramatic happen when I prayed for someone before or since. With God, *ALL* things are possible and He can do *ALL* things!

I giggled, shouted, screamed and praised Jesus all at the same time! I could hardly believe it myself, nor could Pat. He was stunned and sort of stuttered in disbelief. He hadn't seen clearly for years and now instantly he was healed. From that time on, Pat drove everywhere and he became *my* chauffeur, just as I had prayed. He had no vision problems in the least. What a mighty God we serve!

Now, every single thing I was asking God to prove to me that Pat was really the right one, God provided. My prayers had never been answered that swiftly and directly. There was no way around this. This was GOD clearly speaking to me like never before.... yet I was still afraid...

Pat and I continued to work together at the mission where I also lived upstairs. I was very glad to have more men involved in the mission. One outreach that JoAnne my co-worker and I directed, with men assisting, was the 'Under the Bridge Ministry'.

There was an old, deserted underground subway tunnel that had been used sixty years ago in Rochester, NY. It was built next to the Genesee River with many nooks and crannies everywhere; graffiti lined the deserted walls with words I would not ever repeat. Ancient decrepit rooms popped up here and there which once were ticket offices. Spiders wove their cobwebs along the ceilings and down the walls as rats scurried hurriedly through the rubble and over the broken beer bottles- and sometimes over a homeless person's sleeping body.

There were ascending subway steps which had once led to the street above, but now led to nowhere. In this eight-mile tunnel under the city, lay a large platform with immense heating ducts going through the area from the local energy company whose power plant was above. Because of warm air flowing through the ducts which raised the temperature to thirty degrees compared to zero in the winter, many homeless lived on this precarious short stretch of concrete. This area soon became overcrowded in the freezing temperatures. Due to lack of space, some would sleep on the 24-inch ledge which overlooked mounds of broken beer bottles, cans, cigarette butts and discarded syringes fifteen feet below. More than one homeless man had fallen into the squalor and very sadly, one poor fellow had tumbled off backward, breaking his neck and dying a few days later.

So here in this underworld maze lived many homeless with their urine-stained blankets, rag-torn sleeping bags and a few clothes, if they were lucky. It was fairly easy to access the point of entry once one knew where it was located. Everyone on the streets knew about this place nicknamed the 'Hole'. Yes, it truly was a den from the pit of hell. Drugs, alcohol, fights, rapes, murders at times, and witchcraft prevailed down there where even most police officers feared to tread.

So when Pat arrived on the scene, we were very glad to have him lead this outreach. Every Friday evening around 11PM, we would go with a small team of Bible students into the Hole. We would bring sandwiches, coffee, blankets, underwear, socks, candles or flashlights, batteries and Bibles.

One of the hardest things to witness in the Hole was the young women living there. One young woman, Susan, had been living there for months. I had spoken to her at our Friday night coffeehouse and begged her to get out of there. She said she would in only a few days.

The next evening, this beautiful young lady was involved in a street fight and was kicked repeatedly in her abdomen. Someone, trying to help her, gave her some strong pain killers to alleviate her intense suffering. Susan proceeded to mix the pain killers with alcohol which proved to be a deadly combination. I found out about this horrific attack two days later. I rushed to the hospital and after identifying myself, the hospital clerk reluctantly told me that Susan had passed away just a few hours earlier. I wondered, how this could happen to a beautiful 29-year-old woman?

Though there is various assistance available to people in desperate situations, sometimes the disenfranchised fall through the cracks of the system. Others choose to live on the street because there are no social rules they have to live by there—only the *street rules*.

Sadness and grief pierced my heart as I asked Jesus to help me deliver more of His destitute children and not watch them die senselessly anymore. We felt more called than ever to share how to escape from the hellish bondage of Satan. The answer was found only through the saving power of Jesus Christ. Patrick was a living testimony of that power and shared his powerful story often.

The Hole looked very much like a cave when you're walking through it with many passages spreading out in all directions. One would have to bend low many times and sometimes crawl to enter into concealed rooms. Only God Himself knew what went on there. We would arm ourselves with Coleman lanterns and flashlights to guide our precarious paths as we walked oven broken concrete, broken beer bottles, mud and rocks. One night we stumbled upon a very dark and secluded room where two sleeping bags laid among a few filthy clothes. We could sense a real evil in that place, in fact, we could almost taste it. We all felt as though we had entered a room attached to Dante's 'Inferno' itself! Though no one was there at the moment, we prayed fervently for the 'residents' that God would deliver them from this insane lifestyle.

Although there are many sad stories about the people who lived in the Hole or on the streets, there were some great victories too, like the one with a woman named Barb.

Barb came into the Urban Center one evening for our dinner. Her hair was in knots, tangled and sticking straight out. Her body odor and the strong smell of urine made me want to shy away from her. Dirty, oversized men's clothing hung from her worn frame. Her face was weathered with years of abuse, drugs, alcohol and misuse by men. Her wayward lifestyle had surely taken its toll.

I couldn't help but stare at Barbara the first time I saw her eat at the Urban Center. She put her chin down to her plate, opened up her mouth and scooped the food in with her fingers! I was taken aback. I had seen a lot of things, but never someone eating in that manner.

Barbara's father left home when she was only six years old. Life became difficult and Barb started rebelling and drinking by age eleven. Her mother seemed helpless to change her, so by the time she was in her early teens she had been sent to various rehabilitation centers and homes. Restless and wanting freedom in her life, Barb ran away many times to find herself living on the streets where she received a quick education in the seamy side of life. This was the beginning of a pattern of homelessness.

She was able to find employment in factories and restaurant work, but street drugs and hard liquor were taking control of her life more and more. It seemed much easier to live by no rules on the streets. Men used and abused her. The agonies of addiction would crawl up and down her body like red hot fire ants, leaving her unable to even sleep at night. Life went from one downward spiral to another. Another hit that was bad, another man that lied to her again, another stone of rejection. Self-hatred was deeply buried in her heart. After failing attempts to get off the streets of Buffalo, Barb moved to Rochester where one of her new homeless buddies led her to a *safe haven*, where there were no rules—the infamous Hole.

Pat and I went to visit her often in the Hole. Her plot of space to live on was on the platform, about eight by five feet. Her belongings consisted of one change of clothes, that is, if she had not gotten robbed for a while, and a filthy sleeping bag. That was it. Pat and I were so saddened by her destitution. Though we had seen many living down in this pit, her circumstances were the very worst we had ever encountered. She had absolutely no one to care for or love her unless someone wanted to misuse her body for a short while. No, surely that was not love.

Barb seemed attracted by the acceptance she felt and God's unconditional love at the Urban Center. She began coming back. Slowly her countenance and mannerisms changed. Little by little

Barb started gaining hope that she could possibly live a normal life. We felt certain that with prayer and Barb's willingness to surrender her life to Jesus, she would have a new beginning.

Pat, having gone through the welfare-disability process in the past, had an especially heavy burden to see Barb get out of the hell hole where she existed and get on her own two feet. He helped her apply for assistance and within seven to eight months, Barb had her own apartment and even some furniture. She started taking care of her physical needs again, her looks, her apartment and her life. Later she moved to a much nicer apartment in the suburbs.

Though I had lost touch with Barb, years later to my great surprise, I answered the phone one day to hear her saying, "Hello Sandy, this is Barb!" We made a date for lunch and it was a great reunion. She had stayed clean and sober for seven years. Barb became a spiritual daughter to me who grew much in her faith in Jesus, the One who had truly set her free. I am so glad we didn't give up on her when it would have been so easy to do. It is true - never give up on anyone! Later, Barbara and I were able to lead her mother to Jesus; she also told her brother the salvation story and he gladly accepted that before he died. Barbara was a living testimony for her Savior. Sadly, Barbara passed away last year unexpectedly but she now rests in the loving arms of Jesus. I know we will be reunited one day and what a glorious day that will be!

Pat and I continued to see each other. Every Saturday evening when the Urban Center would close after serving at our soup kitchen, we would dash out the door and go to our favorite pizza parlor. Forget the pizza, we just stared into each others' eyes and held hands. Other evenings, we would go to a beautiful overlook at a park in the city while the city lights twinkled below us.

Pat would talk to me about our future while I squirmed and felt totally overwhelmed. It all sounded so good. *Was he for real? Would he make all these promises to me, build up my hopes, and then leave me like others had? O God,* I cried, *tell me what to do. I need to hear Your voice!* As I quieted myself, I would feel God's delight, peace and joy in this relationship and so ever so slowly, we did proceed.

It was now April. We had met in the beginning of January, 2000. One night as Pat was leaving the Urban Center, he squeezed my hand and out of the corner of his mouth said, "Love you." *What did he say?* I thought. *O my gosh! He said he loves me. What do I do?* Pat started telling me he loved me more often. I would just look him in the eyes and smile. I knew if I said those three little words, I was making a commitment to a deeper relationship - possibly even marriage. I just wasn't sure if I was ready for that.

Any spare time we had was spent doing simple things together like miniature golf, movies, hikes and holding each other on secluded park benches. (That was my favorite!) I'll never forget that spring on Oxford Street in the heart of Rochester. By May each year, all the magnolia trees are in full bloom, showing off their brilliant pink buds. So there we were, strolling arm in arm down Oxford, enjoying the gorgeous blooms, but more than that, simply enjoying each other.

Again, Pat told me he loved me. Although I could feel myself blushing, I wanted to respond this time. Somehow, I still wasn't ready to say those three little words. *Aha*, I thought, *this will work.* I peered into Pat's deep blue eyes and said, "Well, I like you intensely, Patrick!" He said, "You like me *intensely?*" He couldn't believe I was so afraid to say 'I love you' and just laughed and laughed. I couldn't help but laugh too. Later we found a park bench around the corner where Pat wanted to talk seriously about our future plans again.

He told me how wonderful our life together would be. After being single nineteen years and only having to cook for myself and only when I absolutely had to, the thought of having to prepare tasty meals every day for him seemed like quite a stretch. I never really enjoyed cooking at all. I thought my next statement might slow him down a little. I said, "You know, Pat, I'm not a good cook at all and I don't even like to cook." He responded, "No problem, I'll take you out to dinner every single night." Well, I guess my little game hadn't worked after all.

Actually, I was relieved that I didn't have to impress him with my cooking. I suppose he might have had a clue anyway. I had only invited him once to join me and some friends to my apartment above the Urban Center for dinner. I think he thought I might prepare him a delicious grand buffet!. Well for me, since I was very frugal, I didn't like to throw anything away. So I proceeded to dig through the Urban Center leftovers from the Saturday night soup kitchen and found there was lots of ostrich burger meat leftover. (Yes, ostrich burger! At the Urban Center, we got accustomed to eating whatever was donated.) I thought that might be delicious with some canned spaghetti sauce. I found out later that Pat wasn't very excited about my menu. Love is blind they say; maybe it dulls your taste buds too!

As the days and weeks passed, Pat and I just had to see each other every day. Everyone who saw me at the Urban Center remarked how radiant and joyful I looked. They said all the stress and strain in my face was gone and my eyes just glistened—like a woman in love. Pat and I would talk for hours on end; we prayed together daily and shared our favorite scriptures. More and more this seemed like a relationship made in heaven by God Himself. Yes, I was starting to believe that he was the one God had for me after waiting all these years.

By June, Pat and I were head over heels in love. As we were spending another romantic evening on a park bench, Pat got very specific about our future and said, "Come on darling, let's get married."

I couldn't directly answer, but I knew through God's guidance plus the love and joy I felt in my heart that: *yes, he was to be my husband*. So I also began to talk about our future and our wedding plans while we held each other tightly. We had agreed not to kiss until we were officially engaged with a ring. Naturally Patrick wanted to get engaged as soon as possible!

I had always wanted a marquise-shaped diamond engagement ring and within a few days, we were shopping in every jewelry store in town looking for the ring beyond compare. It had to be simple, but perfect. Finally we found it at a local mall and Pat and I were so thrilled to see how it sparkled and shimmered on my ring finger. This was *the* one. "OK", Pat said, "You don't get it now. You'll have to be surprised." "All right", I said, that will just make the wait that much more exciting!" After about three weeks, I thought, *well Pat, when are you going to give me my ring anyway?*

June 23, 2000 started out as any ordinary day. Our volunteers would usually arrive early and knock at the back door of the Urban Center to be let in. That morning, I was still upstairs getting ready for the work day ahead when there was a knock downstairs at the door. Whoever it is, they are just way too early, I thought.

My heart quickly warmed as I approached the door and could see through the glass pane that it was Patrick. I swiftly swung open the door, a huge smile on my face. Before I could even say a word, Pat grabbed my hand and knelt down on one knee facing me and said, "Sandy, my love, will you marry me?" He proceeded to pull out a small box from his pocket and opened it to display the beautiful marquise diamond ring we had chosen together. I was overwhelmed.

This was the moment I had dreamed of for the last 19 years. God had always been so faithful in my life; now He was allowing me to live-out my dream. I cried, "Oh yes, Pat, oh yes, I will marry you, I will, I will!" He slipped the ring on my finger and we hugged for what seemed like an eternity. I didn't want that moment to ever end.

After I settled down a little, I asked Pat why he had chosen that dingy doorway to ask me to marry him. He said, "Honey", don't you remember? That is where you and I first met. You opened the door for me there a few months ago and I laid eyes on you for the very first time." That spot instantly turned very romantic!

After announcing the news to a few close friends and coworkers, we both wanted to tell the entire world. We planned to announce our engagement to all the guests we served at our soup kitchen the following Saturday evening, and we did just that. The visitors were so thrilled for us as they let out boisterous shouts of joy and applause. It was such a pleasure to share our joy with all the homeless and needy that we loved so much. Most were very happy, but a few had concerns and questions.

Since they had never seen me date before, much less be in a serious relationship, they assumed I was like a Catholic nun or something. They just assumed I wouldn't or couldn't get married again. One dear fellow said he considered me to be like 'Mother Mary'. I had to laugh and reassure him that I was definitely a normal person and to please take me off his pedestal. And yes, I was allowed to fall in love and even get married. Another visitor, a dear lady of the streets, approached me privately. She had been discussing our good news with another lady of the streets and they were both very worried for me. She asked, "Do you know 'what to do' after you get married?" Again, I had to chuckle and reassure her that yes, I would be just fine. After all, I was 52 years old and had two grown boys of my own!

Pat and I wanted an outdoor wedding and autumn would be here in a blink of an eye. We picked 3 PM on September 24th. That was only three months away and I had so much to do! I had always wanted a very simple wedding but Pat had very different ideas. He thought we should really do it up big and invite everyone we knew and then some. I thought, *the more we invite, the more money it will cost, and we don't have any money.*

As Pat and I talked, he reminded me of how big God is and that He was our provider Who will meet all of our needs. Pat continued to reassure me that it was okay to expand our plans. How could I resist him when he looked at me with such love and joy radiating from his deep blue eyes?

First we had to find a park with an area large enough to hold all our guests. After checking out various parks, we settled on one of the largest in Rochester—Ontario Beach Park. In the middle of the park stood a gigantic gazebo with Lake Ontario and the beach shimmering behind it. I could just picture the two of us standing there in that gorgeous setting exchanging our vows. Below the gazebo was a large area for dancing and seating. This looked like the perfect place for us.

Another concern of ours was choosing a location where the homeless and others could access without cars. Pat and I had decided that we would personally go to all the homeless shelters in town and invite them to our wedding. They would be our 'honored guests' and we wanted to be sure they knew that we really meant that. The fact that this park was on a bus line was a definite plus! I called the city the next day to reserve our date. It was open! Our special day would be coming very soon.

Without any money we needed several miracles to put together such a large wedding. How could we possibly pay for all this? We prayed and prayed and experienced miracle after miracle.

OK, I thought, *how would we pay for all the food?* We wanted it to be nice and really special, but we could only afford to buy ziti, bread and some salad. After more prayer, we decided to include on the invitations to ask guests to bring a side dish, if they could. They did and we had seven baskets of food left over – enough to give to other homeless missions!

O yes, then the invitations. We enlisted the help of a friend to make our wedding invitations on a computer. It even had our picture on it. He would not let us pay for them. We made about 1,500 copies and personally passed them out at the missions as we had planned. We had not any idea how many guests would actually show up, but we were hoping for at least 500. God would surely need to direct every single step.

Sept. 24, 2000
Mr. & Mrs. Patrick Whalen

Next on the list was a photographer. We thought that would probably cost over $1,000, but a dear friend and professional in the field who also served at the Urban Center offered his services free of charge—including the developing and printing of the pictures. This was another answer to prayer.

No wedding is complete without a yummy cake. How would we ever be able to afford a cake big enough for 500 guests? Another friend of mine, Janet who made beautiful wedding cakes, offered to make our cake free of charge. It was designed in many layers spread out so it wouldn't collapse under the weight. Janet told me later that she used 98 eggs and 15 pounds of sugar to make it. Who cares about calories and cholesterol on a special day like this? Not us—that's for sure!

Every woman dreams of the day she will walk down the aisle wearing the most beautiful dress she has ever laid eyes on. Since Pat had inspired me to go all the way on this wedding, a simple dress just didn't seem appropriate as our wedding plans were growing bigger by the minute. The time had come to look at dresses. However, I had very little money in my bank account but I knew God always makes a way.

The money for my dress came from the most unusual place in the world—the IRS! Surprisingly, I had made a mistake on my in-

Sandy singing her love song to Pat at their wedding

come taxes that year. A refund check for $200 from the IRS came at just the perfect time and I knew it was for my dress. Thank you God and Uncle Sam.

I believed that God already had *the* perfect dress picked out for me. I described to the saleslady at the dress shop what I was looking for and before I knew it, she had slipped the dress over my head and zipped it up. I was standing on a pedestal gazing in the mirror. I felt like the most beautiful woman in the entire universe, like a queen, a bride-to-be - madly in love. This was *the* dress and it fit so well too.

I asked the clerk how much it cost and she replied, "$600." My heart quickly sank as I said, "I only have $200; that's all I can spend on this dress." I prayed silently as she said she would ask the owner if they could sell it for less. After seeming like an eternity, the clerk returned and said, "That dress happens to be close-out. We can sell it to you for $200." I could not believe my ears! How I praised my Heavenly Father who is always watching out for us and cares about every detail—right down to a wedding dress for me. I continued to feel God's closeness and joy more and more as our big day drew closer.

For flowers, my friend Diane recommended someone she knew who could design silk flower bouquets. I enlisted her help for a very good price so that was all set, or so I thought.

Next were the plans for a rehearsal dinner. I wanted to plan a simple dinner somewhere with just the wedding party to save money. Patrick said that no, we were to go all out on this also and bless everyone. We found one of the most beautiful restaurants in town overlooking Lake Ontario and a very pricey menu to go with it. I explained to Pat that we could not possibly invite all the 25 people he wanted to come; we would just have to cut back on the guest list. Again, after more prayer, I decided that he was right, as usual, and that somehow God would provide once again.

I called the restaurant and reserved the seating for the extra guests with peace in my heart knowing that God would take care of the situation once again. *Oh God, please come through for us again*, I prayed. Only a few hours later, one of my good friends, Patti, called. I told her of our dilemma, but that we were trusting God. She asked me how many extra persons we had planned to invite to the dinner. It was eleven more. She exclaimed, "Oh that is great, I will pay for the eleven extra myself and that will be my wedding gift to you." I was overwhelmed! God, as usual, had gone beyond my expectations.

Our engagement was a whirlwind of joy and activity plus we still needed to feed and minister to many homeless and needy at the Urban Center at the same time. When I would slow down a little, I wrote thoughts and prayers in my journal. Here are a few excerpts I recorded from this exciting time:

June 12, 2000

I laughed all day with Pat. I never want to leave him. I prayed, 'O Lord, thank You so much for this wonderful, sweet, kind and gentle man You've sent me. He is so awesome and our love is like the love You have for me. I feel so overwhelmed with love.'

June 22, 2000 A 'word' from God to my heart.

O My dear one, you are so precious and valuable to Me. I don't desire your works, but your love. It pleases Me so much when you just love on Me, dance, sing, and rejoice. Yes, I do look and watch over you with joy and rejoicing. It also gives Me much joy to see you and Patrick rejoice over each other, for as you continue your relationship in Me, you honor Me and I will honor you and your marriage.

July 11, 2000

Pat and I are getting married in less than eleven weeks. I can hardly believe it. He is the desire of my heart. So much to plan and do, but GOD will have to do it. We have NO money, but we have GOD and we trust God to provide in every way—abundantly! We are SO in love. I can't wait for the honeymoon! We really do love each other so much. God has been so faithful. I am so thankful to God for the wonderful gift He has given me. Thank you Jesus, for Your faithfulness, love and care. I pray we have the best marriage and relationship of anyone in the world—by Your Spirit! Yes, Lord! (I believe God answered that prayer.)

Last, but not least, Pat wanted to invite almost the entire planet to this wedding! The stress of planning all this was starting to overwhelm me. Pat came to me about one month before the wedding and said, "Let's invite the whole city of Rochester to our wedding." He *was not* kidding.

I almost collapsed. I knew Pat was a man of big dreams, but I thought *how in the world would we do this?* With Pat's love, encouragement and steadfastness that God would work it all out, I finally agreed. We decided to send out press releases about our upcoming wedding to TV stations and newspapers. We were so blessed that the main newspaper in Rochester, The Democrat and Chronicle, included a feature article about our wedding coming in just a few weeks!

After the article was published, Pat got the brilliant idea to put our wedding invitation on huge billboards all around the city. However, I knew that I would be the one to arrange all the details. I threw up my hands and said, "Patrick, I cannot do one more single thing for this wedding if you want your bride alive! If you want billboards, you'll have to handle it all yourself from start to finish, period, the end!" Pat looked at me a little strangely. Well, that was the last I ever heard about any billboards; Pat would just have to settle for the invitation in the newspaper!

For this wedding,
no guest or helper is uninvited

Mr. Patrick Whalen and **Ms. Sandy Huddle** joyfully request the pleasure of your company at their wedding at 3 p.m. Sept. 24 in the bandstand on the beach at Charlotte. The ceremony will be conducted by Pastor **Al Galvano** of Rochester Christian Church.

What's that you say? You don't know this couple? That's no problem. They still want you to attend their wedding.

Patrick, 49, is a volunteer at the Rochester Urban Center, 20 Amherst St., where Sandy, 52, is a director. The two have formed close relationships with many people who are homeless in the city, so when they first began planning a wedding they decided to invite the homeless to join in the festivities.

After distributing 1,500 invitations to homeless people via shelters and 35 city churches, Patrick and Sandy estimated they might have around 500 wedding guests. Then the question of transportation arose, since homeless people usually don't own or have access to cars.

The couple hope someone will volunteer to provide buses to transport those people to the wedding, which is to take place in the bandstand at the beach park.

They also need help preparing and serving a pasta meal after the ceremony.

By extending their invitation to the community at large, Patrick and Sandy believe they may have as many as 2,000 guests.

"I'm in awe," said Patrick, who

CAROL RITTER

Contact her at:
Democrat and Chronicle
55 Exchange Blvd.,
Rochester, NY 14614
258-2309

critter@DemocratandChronicle.com

was a salesman until a carotid artery blockage and a series of mini-strokes left him with a disability and unable to work.

"It's getting bigger than I thought, but we really feel good about this," he said.

Anyone who could help the couple assemble and feed their wedding guests may call Patrick at 226-3327 or Sandy at 461-5329.

This is a second marriage for both. They will be living in Avon, Livingston County.

Wedding In the Park!!!

Sandy & Patrick of the Rochester Urban Center

Everyone Invited to Attend!

We request the honor of your presence
at the sacred union of

Sandra Carol Huddle
to
Patrick James Whalen

On Sunday, the twenty-fourth of September, two thousand
At three o'clock in the afternoon

Ontario Beach Park Gazebo
north of
4791 Lake Avenue, Rochester, New York

Reception immediately following at
Beachfront pavilion in the same park
(chairs optional)

I was getting ready to be married to the man of my dreams, my soul-mate, but life wasn't always like that. I was raised in a strict Roman Catholic home and I loved both my parents very much. My brother Roger was 14 when I was born so I tended to idolize him as I grew up. After all, he was my older and only brother even though he was quite a mischievous teenager, to say the least. My early childhood and teenage years turned out to be very tempestuous for me.

My father worked for the local brewery in St. Louis, Missouri, where I grew up. Many evenings he came home very intoxicated. Unfortunately, my dad would get extremely agitated when he drank and would take it out on my mother. As soon as he would walk in the door the fighting would begin; sometimes it lasted all night. I saw much disturbing violence that a little girl should never see. I would run and hide in the other room to stay out of harm's way. Though my dad was very strict with me, he never abused me and was mostly loving to me and my sister, who was born six years after me.

To my father's credit, when he was sober, he was a wonderful man; a very hard working and fun person. Years later both my mother and father asked God to change their lives and were 'born again by the Spirit', asking Jesus to be their personal Lord and Savior. My dad showed great compassion caring for my mother when she became seriously ill. After her death, Dad started helping the poor and homeless. He would go all over the city five days a week until the age of ninety-one, when he died, and would pick up any leftover food from the grocery stores or the dumpsters if need be, and feed the hungry. Dad even formed his own little team of workers and was awarded a citation from one of the many churches and organizations he served.

In his eighties, he finally and completely stopped drinking. I was so proud of my dad and how he had changed his entire life. I remember him telling me that his later years of helping the poor gave him great joy and they were the happiest years of his life. People do change, sometimes a complete 360 degrees, through prayer and God's intervention. Never give up on anyone.

However, as a little girl, I learned never to make my father angry in any way so I did my best to please him. I became a *people pleaser* to everyone around me for many years and wanted to avoid conflict at any cost. By age sixteen, I had already fallen in love with my first steady boyfriend. He was cute, funny and liked me so I thought that would be all I needed in a husband. We were engaged by my senior year in high school. I thought I was so old at that time. I became a bride at age nineteen, but signs of trouble were brewing even while we were still dating. I remember my fiancé at the time putting his hand through a wall and punching it out because he was angry with me. Another time, he threw a coke bottle at me in anger while we were at a park.

Heavy drinking was pretty much the norm for him, as well as fighting during the drinking parties we both attended. I had my share of alcohol too. I truly believed that once he married me, all this nonsense would stop. I didn't realize that unless God intervened, the addictive and abusive behavior would only escalate. I got pregnant with our first child who was born thirteen months after our wedding. I was now the ripe old age of twenty. By twenty-three, my second son was born.

Though my husband and I loved each other, his violent behavior scared me. There were so many evenings I had dinner prepared, waiting to enjoy it with him, and he wouldn't come home many times till the early morning hours in a drunken stupor, fresh from the bars. I didn't know how to cope with two small children so I would cry my eyes out and then our fighting would begin once he came home. Just like my mom and dad.

Physical and verbal abuse became more frequent. Life had some joys, but the abuse took its toll. By the eighth year of our marriage, I sought counseling; I just wanted to be happily married. The chaplain I went to actually suggested a divorce if my husband wasn't willing to get any help. My children were still small so I could not even imagine doing that; I still loved him!

Years passed; the boys grew up, but the abuse of all types only increased. After fourteen years, my love and patience had grown thin. I felt numb inside and didn't even know what I felt anymore. I had shut down my emotions a long time before. Finally, I told my husband that either we get counseling together or I would file for divorce. We did make a few attempts, but it didn't seem to help us. We didn't know where else to turn and really didn't have a clue as to how to fix our marriage. The sad thing is that we both still had some love for each other. We tried a separation. Things went all right for three months after that, but soon all the old patterns emerged. We never even once thought to pray and ask God to help us, though we attended church every Sunday.

The abuse and violence intensified more after the separation. In desperation, I told my husband I wanted a divorce and we were granted a no fault divorce in April, 1983. I had very mixed feelings about all this, but at this point, I just wanted *out*.

My sons were stunned. We moved from our home and their school district to a small apartment close to my family. It was a colossal blow to all of us. It took about three months for the reality of what I had done to sink in. When it finally did, I became upset, depressed, lonely and felt totally abandoned. The pressure of trying to raise two sons with one less salary was extremely hard. Everything as I knew it had changed abruptly. I even had to sell my little dog, Benji, as I couldn't afford the extra rent for him. Enough money at the end of the month was a thing of the past.

Since I had pursued a no fault divorce, my husband and I had settled on an amount of child support for our children that was far below what I actually needed, as I realized later.

I started not liking myself, my life or my circumstances. My head would literally swirl in confusion as I would cry myself to sleep every night. Life seemed to get darker and darker and much more difficult. My sons also had their own reactions to the divorce. The older would let it all out and had much trouble in school and at home. His emotions would boil up over the top which only caused more heartache for us all. My younger, rather than explode, pushed all his emotions deep down inside and became very quiet and withdrawn. I could not understand either one of them. I felt helpless, confused and alone.

Though I was still a churchgoer, I did not know how to pray, or that it was even possible to reach a loving God. He seemed too distant and far removed from my problems to ever help me. No one seemed to care. Loneliness wrapped its arms around me and gripped me tight. I could not live like this. Surely someone out there was just waiting for me and I would find a really wonderful new husband, or so I thought. Yes, there was someone waiting for me all right, but it was not at all what I had bargained for.

I visited a few singles' groups looking for the man of my dreams. Well, I'd meet a guy, then another guy, and another. They were waiting for me—to see what I could give them and how they could use me.

After a few months, I fell head over heels in love with Joe. We dated and had a passionate affair for almost one year. I thought I wanted to marry him. He was the first person to tell me he loved me after many years. It all felt so good. We partied and danced in the bars and woke up together in the mornings when my kids weren't around.

However, there was a side of him I couldn't quite uncover. It seemed as if something was hidden—and it was. After months of him telling me things that just didn't add up, I met his daughter one day and she spilled the beans. Her father, she said, was a chronic alcoholic, was seeing other women behind my back and to top it off, was a compulsive liar. Now all these unexplained paradoxes made sense. I was in a state of shock. This could not be true. I had been so in love that I couldn't see the deception right in front of my own eyes. I quickly confronted Joe, but of course, he denied everything. I told him we would have to separate for thirty days so I could get my head on straight. Slowly, I came down from my cloud and realized that all these things were true and that I had been duped by a gigolo who was taking me for all he could get.

I was devastated. I was starting to realize how the single scene was nothing more than a *meat market*. People were after whatever they could get to make themselves feel better. Forget the other person. Sex, drugs and booze, that's where it was at. At least that was what was offered to me as an answer for all my pain. Anger and disappointment grew inside me till I could not control it. I just had to have a lover now, no matter what the cost. I just didn't care. *OK, maybe I am a loser now,* I thought. *I'll get what I can from anyone, party fast and furious. Life like this doesn't really matter anyway and neither do I.*

I was experiencing unbelievable inner turmoil. I didn't know at the time I was falling right into the plan of the enemy himself—the devil. His plan was to have me end my life quickly and end up in hell with him forever.

My lifestyle in the next one and one-half years went from bad to worse. I was on a dark path of self-destruction. I was always looking for the right man; with one affair after affair. *Maybe the next one,* I reasoned, *would love me for who I was and not for what I could provide.* I was wrong, so wrong. My loneliness and hopelessness only grew. I was often out in the evenings until early morning partying while my boys had to fend for themselves. By this point, I was just hoping they could handle themselves because I was too mixed up to even try. Another lover seemed interested in me for a while, maybe we would really get serious. Months later, he and my best friend announced that they were seeing each other behind my back and were planning to get married!

I now really started hating myself, my life and what I had become. I was no longer the nice mom who was married with two kids and went to PTA meetings. I had turned into a sex addict and had absolutely no way to stop. Life became a blur.

After another short interlude with another lover, I realized right before he left that I actually did not have enough money for food for my kids in the morning. I asked him if I could borrow a few bucks. He angrily threw $10 on my table as he left. I picked it up and realized that I had just gotten paid for my services. Shame and disgust started to rise up in my gut. I cried myself to sleep, just like so many other nights. I never saw the guy again. I started to question myself, *where did I go? What has happened to Sandy?*

Such extreme anguish was building up inside of me that I thought I might explode. Nothing or no one could really satisfy me. No one was quenching my deep desire to be loved just the way I was, for who I was. Unconditional love without strings attached was not in anyone's vocabulary that I knew. I was on a deadly journey searching frantically everywhere for true love but I had no idea if I would ever find it. I loved my two sons, but I knew that I was not being a good mother anymore. Somehow I was able to hold a job even though I got very little sleep most nights from my party lifestyle. I felt like I was always on a merry-go-round. I was up when I had lovers and down when they ditched me. This cycle repeated itself over and over again. I couldn't possibly continue like this.

The answer, I thought, was *more* of the same: more booze, more parties and more men. If I died, I died, so what? I would find men anywhere and everywhere. I was not going to be lonely anymore. I would show all of them. I tried so very hard to do just that. Now I was actually the one who could walk in any bar and pick up a guy and made sure he came home with me that night. That was all I needed. I was digging another notch deeper into my own living hell. Life didn't seem worth living at all.

Enter some good friends. A few of my girlfriends saw my life-style and were very concerned for me. They started inviting me to Bible studies. I refused over and over and would laugh and say, "I'm the party animal of our group, remember? No way will I go to a Bible study." They persisted over and over. Finally, to shut them up, I agreed to go, but only if we could go drinking afterward. For many months I went to various Bible studies and then enjoyed the bars afterward. After all, I had reasoned, didn't Jesus drink? I secretly made fun of the group moderator and would ask ridiculous questions to throw the leader off. I thought I was being very coy and a real know-it-all. I laugh now.

God saw through my prideful and self-righteous attitude as well as a multitude of other sins, and saw my broken and wound-ed heart. He neither judged nor accused me. How God put up with me, I'll never know. I deserved to be in hell and never know His love, or anyone else's for that matter. I laughed at God back then, but He saw my pain and wept with me. At the Bible stud-ies I could pretend to be a good girl for a few hours and then go on with my wretched lifestyle later. After all, it made my friends happy that I was going and I needed to keep a few good friends.

However, God's Word eventually started piercing my heart, though I was not willing to admit it. I could feel a stirring, a drawing to Him. *What was that?* I thought. My girlfriends started telling me more about Jesus and how He could set me free from my terrible lifestyle and give me eternal life plus the true love, peace and joy that I was so craving. Still with a rebellious heart,

I continued on my fast-paced road to destruction. I just knew I would find the right man and he would make me happy like no one else had.

Finally, I did meet a very nice young man who seemed like he would possibly marry me and be a really good husband; *that was the answer to all my problems,* I thought. Apparently, his ex-wife became jealous when she found out we were getting serious. On the sly, he started seeing his ex-wife while we were still dating. After another passionate evening, this nice young gentleman announced to me that he was going back to his ex-wife; they were to be re-married. My heart was crushed; I didn't think I could take anymore. I had become a commodity for anyone who would only ask. I was just there for the taking.

Heartbroken and shocked, I returned home before dawn, with eyes red and face swollen from hours of crying. I had finally reached the end of it all. I was sick of myself. I was sick of my actions and the party lifestyle, of all the men who had used and abused me, of life. I had nothing left in me anymore. I searched for answers in my mind, but found none. How could I go on any longer?

But there was one way out, I thought. I'll end my life; just kill myself. I could just take an overdose of sleeping pills and never wake up again. It would be very quiet and painless and finally all be over. At the time it felt very tempting and enticing. I didn't realize that Satan himself was telling me all these lies about suicide in order to get my soul in hell for eternity. Frankly, I didn't know what I believed anymore.

As I pondered thoughts of suicide over and over, the words of my friends' encouragements about Jesus began to drift through my mind. I remembered many discussions with my friend Mary about how to get to heaven. I had insisted that I was a good person and I would make sure I did enough good works to get there. She would smile and say, "There is no way you can earn your way to heaven. Salvation is only through Jesus Christ and what He alone did for you on the cross."

I told her to prove it, and she led me to the scripture (Ephesians 2:8-9) (NIV): *"For it is by grace you have been saved through faith,— and this not from yourselves, it is a gift of God—not by works so that no one can boast."*

I read it with my own eyes and was shocked. So, no matter how good I was, it wasn't going to earn me a way into heaven. I just could not understand that. My friends had also told me that Jesus told a Pharisee in the Bible that, *"... unless one is born again (born again anew from the Spirit above) he cannot see the kingdom of God (John 3:3)."* I needed to be born again, she said.

She explained that I needed to repent of my sins and turn my life completely over to Jesus. I was to make *Him* my Lord and Savior, *not* my boyfriends or lifestyle or my own rebellious will. I would have to surrender my life to God and follow His ways.

I believe because of their prayers God was drawing me, even right at that very moment. There was an intense battle going on for my soul and my life. Was it really true what my friends had told me? I broke down again and cried. How could I know if God was really there or really existed? Could He really deliver me and change my life? As I curled up in a ball on my living room floor, I thought Jesus might be the only way left. After all, I had just about tried everything else. I knew nothing else worked.

In total desperation, I cried out to God. "Jesus", I screamed, "save me or I die! I don't know if You even exist, but if You do, come and change my life now! I can't live like this anymore. If You really are God, come change me!"

That was it. It was not a fancy prayer, but it was a sincere one, straight from my heart. My crying slowly subsided and my thoughts of suicide instantly vanished. Peace filled my heart and by the next morning, I felt like there was definitely a change in my life. I really had decided to follow Jesus. I was not sure what that entailed, but I was through with the old life. I knew that I would need a lot of help to now live for Jesus.

Since I had been a devout Roman Catholic as a child and attended 12 years of parochial schools, I believed I could never ever leave the church of my upbringing. They had all the truth and a lot of things in other religions were simply not correct. I wanted to protect myself from any false doctrine, so I began for the first time in many years to read the Bible. I wanted to make sure it was the Catholic edition only. As I read, though I didn't understand too much of what I was reading, bells started to go off in my head. Some passages just began jumping off the page. I was a new creation in Christ now and God's Holy Spirit was opening my spiritual eyes for the first time.

I marveled at things I had never understood before. This corresponds exactly to what Paul wrote in the Bible in the book of 1 Corinthians 2:14: *"The man without the Spirit does not accept the things that come from the Spirit of God, for they are foolishness to him and he cannot understand them, because they are spiritually discerned."* (NIV).

Until I had totally surrendered to God and accepted His Son, Jesus, I could not understand much of anything my friends had been telling me. I had to surrender to God by faith and then a whole new spiritual world opened up to me!

One night while I was in my bedroom talking to God, I asked Him to show Himself to me somehow. Suddenly as I looked up at my bedroom door, I saw a vision right before my eyes. A huge seed was covering the length of my door and bright rays of light were streaming out of the seed! I had never seen anything like that in my life! In my heart, I knew that that was a sign from God that He wanted to let me know He was real and heard my little prayers. Little did I know at the time that Jesus is called the Light of the World (John 1:9) and that a seed represents God's Holy Word (Luke 8:11).

I realized right then I still had so much to learn. This 'light' that I saw was starting to pierce my broken and battered heart. For the very first time I realized that there might be a huge world of undiscovered truth or maybe even a huge God that I had never known before due to my own pride and self-righteousness. My curiosity grew and I wanted to know this Jesus more than just saying a five-second prayer to rescue me, even though at the time I had meant every word of it. There had to be more – and there was!

Sandy & Pat falling in love

Pat with his daughters

Sandy age 16

Our wedding day, Sept. 24, 2000

Pat as a new US Marine!

Singing my love song to Pat at our wedding!

Sandy with her sons, 1984

Pat's baptism while serving time in NY

Where Pat & Sandy met - the Rochester Urban Center

'Women of Restored Destinies' Support Group, Rochester

Pat made it! Elim Bible Institute Graduation, 2005

Saturday night service at the Rochester Urban Center

Pizza party in the park outreach, Rochester, NY

Ministering to the kids in Kenya

Pat with a leper in Kenya

Children praying after ministry, Calcutta, 1993

In remote Nepal distributing Bibles, 1992

Surrounded by village kids, Calcutta, India

Sandy with her sister, Dad & brother, 1990

Pat preaching in Nairobi, Kenya

Sandy with Barb from the 'hole'

Sandy praying during a street outreach, St. Louis

Pat with his bone marrow doctor, Dr. 'V' (center)

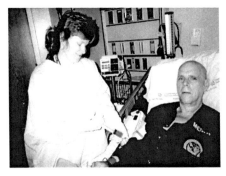

Pat receiving his transplant, Nashville, 2002.

My hunger for God and to know Him much more intimately grew in leaps and bounds. Now I was in church every time the doors were open. I started reading my Bible and setting aside a special time for prayer daily. I began to hear God's voice more and more. What an exciting time that was. Everything was new. My perspective of the whole world had changed. God had given me joy. Life still was hard and money tight, but now I had Christian friends that could listen to me and strengthen me in my new faith. I took baby steps in faith and went through many trials and tests along the way. With God's help, many times I won the battles, but during the first year especially, I lost quite a few too.

Since I had been so addicted to men, my old nature still rose up inside of me often and many times I gave in to the sin that so easily tempted me in my past. I would come home feeling ashamed and guilty before God—and I was. Of course He still loved me but I still had to make hard choices as to who would I really serve. Would I remain a Christian or just forget it all and live to please my flesh?

Though temptations were strong, I knew by this time I really did know and love God and it made me sad to know I had hurt Him and sinned against Him. The only answer was to ask for His forgiveness. His Word says He always will forgive us if we come to Him with a sincere heart. 1 John 1:9 says, "*...that if we confess our sins, He is faithful and just to forgive us our sins and purify us from all unrighteousness.*" God continued to forgive me whenever

I asked Him; I cried out to Him to change me from the inside out as I knew I certainly could not change myself.

It was a process. Some are transformed instantly when they receive Jesus as their Savior, but for many it is a process that they choose to consent to every single day. The battles raged on but finally after one year, I was free of my sex addiction and more in love with Jesus than ever. After a few years, I became involved with a large Christian singles group and became their outreach leader. I wanted everyone to know how Jesus could set them free. If He could do it for me, He could do it for anyone.

Another Christian singles group was organizing a large outreach to Jamaica but I had never dreamed of leaving the United States to share my new faith in Jesus. But now, five years after I had surrendered to Jesus, I went, though I admit that it was with much fear and trembling. Though it was only one week long, God's Spirit so moved me with compassion and joy while I was there that I was hooked for life. I knew I would never be the same. I went on more outreaches to Mexico and other countries. I realized that this was the calling of God on my life, to serve Him full-time and share His mighty life-changing Word everywhere I went, even if it meant to the ends of the earth. Thus began my worldwide trek for Jesus.

Three years after my first mission outreach, I sold almost everything I owned, left my family and two children, who were now grown, and at the age of forty enrolled in a one-year missionary training school with Youth With A Mission in Arkansas. I needed to raise all my funds for schooling and all my daily living. We could not work because our training was full-time. As I shared my need, I saw God provide abundantly for me in every way. He provided so much that I was able to pay the entire first year of school on my first day of class. Living by faith was very challenging, yet it was such a joy to see God's hand going before me in every way. That training took me to Mexico and El Salvador for months at a time. Though leaving family, friends and a good career which I loved was very difficult, the joy of giving the rest of my life to God to do *anything* He asked seemed only a privilege. I remembered clearly where I had been and where my soul was headed before I came to Christ. To serve Him full-time was the least I could do.

After my one-year training, I heard the Lord calling me, of all places, to Calcutta, India with Youth With A Mission. I made a two-year commitment with them. I'll never forget entering that city for the first time and riding on a rickshaw to my new home and assignment. Though I hoped other trips would have prepared me, nothing prepared me for what I saw. This was a radically different culture, many street beggars, homeless children, extreme poverty, statues to Hindu gods and temples on almost every corner while lepers begged for rupees with outstretched nubs for fingers concealed in adhesive taped hands.

My mind went into overload. How would I possibly stay here for two years and survive? However, I slowly did adjust and eventually pioneered Bible classes for Muslim and Hindu street children in the slums of Calcutta. I grew to love the country and especially the children. I played the guitar and learned songs in their language; so many times rows of little street urchins would follow me around the streets and we would sing God's songs together. Afterward, I would take them to get some rice and dal at a local restaurant. They were always so hungry for love and attention more than anything. Even a simple kindness would put huge smiles on their dirt-streaked faces.

At the end of my first year I became seriously ill and I had no idea what was wrong. I literally could not hold my head up as I had lost so much blood. Reluctantly, I went to the Assembly of God Hospital to get an exam and immediately I was admitted. I was terribly low on blood and they put out a call – even on the streets, for donations of blood for me. This was not like in the United States, blood had to be donated for you right then if it was needed. There were no storage labs. Finally some friends were a close match and I went into surgery to remove a very large necrotic tumor from my uterus. They performed a total hysterectomy through my 104-degree fever. The toxins from the dying tumor could have killed me so it was urgent they remove it. I had five pints of blood with O positive and O negative blood as they were in such a hurry to save my life.

In the midst of going through the surgery, little did I know what God was doing behind the scenes. I didn't realize how critical my condition was. I found out one month later that during my surgery which happened to be in the middle of the night in the United States, my friend, Mary Ann, was awakened from sleep by the Holy Spirit. She felt a very strong urge to pray for me, which she did. I am a living testimony today that God answers prayer. I might not be here today had she not obeyed the Holy Spirit and prayed for me. I did wonder at one time if I would come out of the hospital alive, but God reassured me by a Bible verse that quckly popped into my mind, John 11:4: *"This sickness will not end in death. No, it is for God's glory so that God's Son may be glorified through it."*

Though I had many severe complications to deal with after the surgery, including blood poisoning which was not treated at all, I was released to go home seventeen days later and went back to work in the ministry. God's saving hand was truly on me to spare my life for He knew I had a lot more work to do for Him.

Living in Calcutta was one of the hardest things I have ever done, and yet one of the most rewarding also. I would not trade that experience for anything. To see little homeless children and their moms (most were prostitutes) accept Jesus was a joy in my life and it made my commitment to serve Him only more worth it.

Because of my visa situation, I had to leave the country every six months to renew it. Nepal was a short plane ride away just north of India. I had the thrill of resting in Katmandu, Nepal and trekking in the Himalayan Mountains within a few miles of the

Tibetan and Bhutan borders. I was able to distribute Bibles in the Tibetan language to people who had never heard the name of Jesus before. My friend who hiked with me could speak a little Tibetan and Nepalese, so we shared the Gospel as best we could. I always came back to Calcutta tired and sore, but full of joy and refreshed from seeing life from the Himalayan Mountains, which is the highest mountain range in the world. I consider it a great honor to have been called to these places, and I was ready to minister in India for the rest of my life, if that's where the Lord wanted me.

Not long after I made that commitment in my heart, I felt I was being called in a new direction: Bible school. The thought just would not go away. Looking back, I can see God's hand in that direction now. It is so important that we obey Him in everything He calls us to do. If I had disobeyed God at this point, I would not have met Patrick, the love of my life. God sees the future. For me, God has never led me in a straight line. There are tons of twists and turns and roadblocks too, but that just makes our lives more interesting and exciting, doesn't it? Life is certainly never dull when God is our Master.

Was God really asking me to leave Calcutta and His street kids? Through more prayer and confirmations, I believed God was really calling me back to the US after my two-year commitment ended in India. The thought of choosing a Bible school was a little overwhelming so I decided I would go to a good one in Dallas, Texas where some of my friends had gone. How was God going to tell me exactly which one to attend? There were hundreds. I received the school's application while in India and was planning to send it in as soon as I arrived in the States.

But God had an entirely different plan. My main airline stop on the way home was Maui, Hawaii. Are you ready for another miracle? There was a Youth With a Mission base there where I could experience some *reverse culture shock* and R&R before returning to the US. Friends who had visited Calcutta from this

mission base had encouraged me to stop there on my way home -
whenever that would be. I remember booking my trip in Calcutta
and explaining to the travel agent I wanted to stop in Maui for
eight days on the way to the States for the same price. He looked
bewildered and said that of course, was impossible and it would
cost at least $500 more to do that. I said that God would make
a way and to do whatever he could. He left a little flustered to
make phone calls while I sat in his office and prayed for the ten
minutes he was gone. He came back in the office shaking his head
and said, "I don't understand it, but the airline just said you can
do that for just one rupee more (four cents!) How I thanked the
Lord. I knew He had heard my prayers and answered them again.

While in Maui, I was telling one of my new friends there that
I was going to attend a Bible school in Texas. Immediately, the
Holy Spirit pierced my heart and mind and I heard, "How can
you tell her you're going there? You haven't even prayed about it!"
I knew that was true and felt very convicted. I went off by myself
to pray right away as I knew God had more to tell me. As I qui-
etly prayed in the Spirit, the word 'Elim' just popped out of my
mouth. I wasn't sure at all what it was, much less if it was even a
Bible school. However, I was very anxious to find out what Elim
was when I arrived back in my hometown, St. Louis, Missouri.

I found a missionary friend who was knowledgeable in many
areas and I thought he might be able to help me. I asked him if
he knew if there was an Elim Bible School, or anything close to
that anywhere in the US. He said, "Yes, there was. It was an excellent
school called Elim Bible Institute near Rochester, NY." I told him
that was great but I would *never ever* go to New York. I'd live in
India first! Again, I could not get away from God's prodding. This
time I was going to pray seriously about which Bible school to attend. Over and over, God confirmed to me that Elim Bible Institute was the school I was to attend. Without even knowing very
much about the school, I sent in my application to Elim and was

accepted. Three months later I started my first year of their three-year program in Lima, NY, 25 miles south of Rochester, NY.

I knew I was in the center of God's will, though I had no idea what lie ahead. I knew God's plans for me were for good, *to give me a future and a hope* (Jeremiah 29:11). Bible school was a giant challenge for me as I had hours and hours of studying, papers to write, outreaches and more, yet it also gave me great joy. Those three years restored my soul after seeing extreme destitution and hardship in India and living in the middle of it. I needed that time to find new strength in the Lord to prepare for my next assignment. I had no clue what that would be. I wondered, *where oh Lord, will You send me after graduation, what then?*

The preparations were all made for my big day, or so I thought. Patrick and I were to be married in just one short day. My bridesmaids had all arrived. Some had come from out of town and we were ready to celebrate. It was time to pick up the wedding flowers. I gave the money to Judy, my maid of honor, and off she and my bridesmaids went to get the artificial bouquets.

I had had some doubts about the flowers all along. Whenever I would call the woman who was designing them, she always gave me very vague answers, but assured me that they would be ready in time. I had cautioned Judy to make sure that everything was correct and done beautifully as ordered before she paid for them. I then busied myself with more duties as the bride-to-be and didn't see my bridesmaids until the wedding rehearsal dinner hours later.

As we were walking into the restaurant for our dinner, I couldn't wait to ask Judy how my flowers looked. She said, "Oh Sandy, you wouldn't believe it. The designer hasn't even started on *any* of your bouquets yet and said that she would be gone most of the day, but she promised she would have the flowers ready by tomorrow!"

Neither Judy nor I were going to buy that line. My heart sank as I wondered what we would possibly do for flowers in just a few hours.

Judy then said, "Don't worry. God already has done a miracle."

"Really?" I exclaimed! Oh, how I needed to hear that. Judy said that she picked up all the loose artificial flowers from my designer and she and the bridesmaids went to find help anywhere they could. They stopped to pray and ask God's direction as they knew this could be a serious problem for a wedding.

Soon they were standing in a local fabric and floral shop. Judy explained to the clerk the terrible dilemma and asked if there was any way she could help. As they were talking, the clerk was actually making a bouquet and when Judy finished, the clerk asked, "You mean like this?"

"Oh yes," Judy said, "that would be so lovely!"

The clerk said that that was no problem and she would make all of the bouquets for the bride, five bridesmaids plus all the other flowers needed and would have them ready by the next day –my wedding day! The cost would only be $75. Such a low price for so much was unheard of.

Sure enough, my bridesmaids picked the flowers up the next day and they all were as beautiful as promised. Who knows, maybe the clerk was an angel on special assignment; I would like to think so. In any case, she definitely was an angel to me.

Sunday, Sept. 14, 2000. I woke up with joy and excitement exploding in my heart. This was the day. It all seemed so surreal. I had waited so long and in just a few hours I would be married to the love of my life. *The weather?* I thought. *What if it rains?* I peered out my window to see if it was overcast or starting to rain. It was. Our wedding was going to be outside so it just could not rain. That was not an option. I jumped out of bed and started praying for a beautiful, sunny day. "Oh God," I cried, "We need a miracle today. Please stop the raindrops and let the sun shine bright!"

Little by little the rain stopped and the clouds parted to make room for the glorious sun. There were only a few hours remaining before the wedding. My spiritual daughter, Liz, drove me to the site of the ceremony, Ontario Beach Park to get ready to walk down the 'aisle'. The aisle was 300 feet of grass leading up to the gazebo. We parked far away from the crowds so I wouldn't be seen before my walk down the aisle. The clock was ticking. It was

3 PM, time to begin. As I got out of Liz's car, a local TV crew jumped in front of me to interview me about the wedding and our involvement with the homeless. I found out later three TV stations filmed our wedding and clips of it were shown on all the stations.

I could hear my friend Gene on his trumpet and his wife Cathy on the keyboard, preparing to play the famous wedding march, Paschelbel's *Canon in D Major* for my entrance. My heart was leaping out of my chest as my dad approached and said now it was the time to take our famous walk. Arm in arm, Dad and I strolled down the path. I gazed around to see hundreds of my friends, including many homeless, standing up and clapping as we approached the gazebo. Dad was amazed and said, "Sandy, this is not a wedding, this is an event!" I couldn't help but chuckle. I realized I was experiencing more than I could ever ask for or imagine. This was over the top! Again God's Word was coming to pass as it says in Ephesians 3:20: *"Now to Him who is able to do exceedingly abundantly above all that we ask or think, according to the power that works in us…"*

As I looked ahead, I could see that from the center of the gazebo ceiling there hung a beautiful four-by-six-foot white and gold banner. Embroidered on it was the scripture: *Let us rejoice and be glad and give Him glory! For the wedding of the Lamb has come and His bride has made herself ready.* (Revelation 19:7). That verse speaks of our union with Jesus Himself, the Lamb of God in Heaven as all the saints, the Bride of Christ, will gather together for the consummation of the ages. Marriage on earth is a foreshadowing of this and Pat and I would become one in this holy union in just a few moments.

Now as I drew closer, I could see Patrick staring at me with eyes of tenderness, love and joy. I couldn't stop smiling. I wanted this moment to last forever. I slowly walked up the steps to the gazebo. My father placed my hand in Pat's and kissed me on the cheek, then turned and walked away. For the next hour we held hands tightly as we pronounced our sacred vows, exchanged rings and received prayer from pastors and friends.

Judy, my maid of honor, surprised us with a beautiful poem she had written for the occasion and read it during the ceremony. To surprise Pat, I sang a love song to him accompanied by my guitar that God had given me a few weeks earlier. I didn't know if I could possibly do that on such a momentous occasion, but with God's help, I sang of my love to God and Patrick with all I had inside me. I watched Pat's eyes moisten and his heart melt.

Parts of the ceremony were quite humorous too. Many of our homeless friends had cigarettes hanging out of their mouths during the wedding. Pat and I were glad it wasn't vodka bottles, so we were okay with that. Also, our homeless friends were quite excited for both of us and cheered us on loudly during the ceremony at times. When the officiating Pastor would take a little break in speaking, we could hear from the crowd, "Go girl, go! That's my girl! Yahoo you two" or some other variation of that. Pat and I felt their love and encouragement and though not very proper, we didn't care in the least. Our friends were there to celebrate with us and that's all that really mattered.

Toward the end of the ceremony, Pat and I turned around and faced the crowd of 500. We saw family, friends, the homeless and needy and many we didn't even know as they had come because of the invitation in the paper. We shared God's joy, love and plan of salvation with them and invited them to come forward right then and there to receive God through His Son Jesus. Twenty-five people came forward! What a joy to see many becoming one with Christ in a new relationship just as Pat and I were beginning a new union with each other on this special day.

Now it was time to walk back down the aisle as husband and wife. I had never felt such joy in my entire life and I didn't know if I could contain it all. Pat and I loved each other with a love that was ordained in Heaven itself. I could feel God's joy and pleasure over us. The worship team began to sing this joyous song as we danced back down the aisle. I tweaked the words slightly to adapt for this day:

Look what the Lord has done.
Look what the Lord has done.
God gave her a husband; God gave him a wife.
They'll love together the rest of their lives.
Oh I'm going to praise His name.
Each day He's just the same.
Come on and praise Him; look what the Lord has done!

We danced away the rest of the day at our outdoor reception with hundreds of our guests. We ate until we couldn't eat one more bite. We served up all the delicious wedding cake and laughed like crazy when one of our guests lifted up an eight-foot metal park bench and actually balanced it on his chin. We longed for evening to come when we could slip off to begin our one-month honeymoon. My dream had become true. I had now become Mrs. Patrick Whalen, the happiest woman in the world.

After our honeymoon, Pat and I continued to serve the poor at the Rochester Urban Center. We were there most days cooking, serving, preaching or talking and counseling with the many needy folks there. Pat was a visionary and felt God had given him many plans and ideas on how to expand the ministry to reach more hurting people. I stood by his side and cheered him on. Pat was also looking very forward to starting Elim Bible Institute in the spring semester, which would be in just a few months.

Pat and I worked, laughed, prayed and worshipped together and our love grew deeper and sweeter. Though our first year had some small bumps along the way, we always worked our differences out quickly through prayer and communication. We never had a serious argument. Pat and I had become a team that was knit together in heart and spirit. There was never a doubt in our minds that God had truly established our lives together. Our joy in serving others and each other increased and life seemed as though it couldn't get any better.

By July of the following year, we organized a medical outreach to Kenya with a nurse friend of ours, Diane. We had met some Kenyan pastors at our Bible school and they had asked us to come and help them for one month, which we were very eager to do. With excitement and anticipation, the three of us flew to Nairobi, Kenya, in July, 2001, where we were whisked off to lead a three-day crusade in a large church. We were given no notice about these meetings. We needed God more than ever! God answered our prayers and brought His Holy Spirit to the meetings along with His joy, peace and deliverance.

For the next two weeks we ministered in towns and villages, preaching outdoors. There was no electricity in these villages, so we reasoned that a sound system could not be used for our meetings, but the locals had it all figured out. A few antiquated cars made it up the steep mountains and hills. We weren't sure what was going to happen as they opened the hood of one of their cars and disconnected the battery cables. Soon, they had hooked up a sound system to the battery and were playing their electric guitars—loudly. They gave us a microphone to preach with and we were able to minister. We had many joys as we shared the Good News of Jesus with the villagers as well as hundreds of playful children that surrounded us daily, waiting for a hug or a piece of sweet candy.

We also joined with three local doctors who helped us run medical outreaches in their villages. We were able to treat and see hundreds each day at the clinics. Malaria was a huge killer in these areas. Though malaria is fairly easy to treat, many were dying in the bush due to no hospital close by and/or no money to pay for even basic treatment. How we wished we could stay and do so much more! Pat and I decided on this trip that we would definitely go back as full-time missionaries for at least one year after he graduated from Bible School.

One day, Diane and I had the privilege of working with the international organization Compassion International, a Christian aid group that helps thousands of suffering children in third world countries. We were asked to screen children for certain conditions. For one screening, we were to inspect underneath their eyes for anemia.

I kept passing all the kids along as fine while Diane, the nurse, found that about 50% of her group needed medical attention. After about two hours, she asked me exactly what I was doing. Needless to say, I had totally misunderstood the directions Diane had given me. I was so embarrassed when I realized Diane would have to tell the director that my entire group would have to be re-inspected for anemia. Since Diane had said to see if the children's eyelids were white or pink, I had every child close their eyes and found that their eyelids were all pink, which is good, I thought. I didn't hear her say the *bottom* eyelid, which is directly under the eye. I didn't even know that was called an eyelid! Though we both felt sorry about what had happened, we rolled in laughter when we both realized what I had done. We still giggle to this day about my blunder.

While flying back to Rochester, NY in a 737 jumbo jet over Europe, suddenly I started to get warm, very warm in fact. In minutes, my body was shaking uncontrollably and wouldn't stop. I quickly developed a fever and the shaking continued off and on throughout the flight. I felt very ill. Finally we landed and I was so glad to be back in the US and wanted to find out quickly what my problem was. My thought was malaria as we discovered we had worked in a high malaria area and had not taken any medi-cine to prevent it. (We had been informed we would not be in a malaria zone.) After going to the doctor and receiving blood tests, I was told it was not malaria. However, even if malaria doesn't show up positive in tests, one can still have the condition.

My symptoms only grew worse. For a few days I would be symptom free and then the fever and violent shaking would start all over again. Finally after seeing a physician friend, I be-gan treatment for malaria and within a few days was fine. Un-fortunately, malaria can hide in your bloodstream and return at any time. Three months later all the symptoms returned. Since it is unheard of in the States, no one wanted to treat me for malaria. After much pleading and praying, I was finally able to obtain the anti-malarial medicine I needed and was better within three days. It has never returned. How I thank God for that!

A few months later, Pat and I organized an outreach to New York City with friends from our church to pray and minister to many hurting people. It was only two months after the devastating attack on New York and the Twin Towers, September 11, 2001. Our first awareness that we were getting close to the site was on the night we arrived. We had taken the subway close to the location. After exiting the subway, we took the steps to the sidewalk above where immediately our nostrils were met with the stench of death and destruction in the air. My stomach did a flip-flop. Then we rounded the corner there and saw first-hand the terrible desolation in front of us. Small plumes of smoke still rose out of the rubble. The site had been barricaded, yet we were able to get fairly close. Great sadness and grief rose up inside of me.

It was hard to comprehend that this horrendous act had happened on our own land to innocent people. My eyes welled up with tears as anger and questions of 'why' filled my heart. The smell was pungent and sickening. There was no reason. We gathered together as a team and cried and prayed for the families that had lost loved ones. We also prayed for the perpetrators and their families; we asked God for grace to forgive them in our hearts. My perspective of life was changed that day and I will never be the same after being there for that very sad and sobering moment.

Thousands of people had come to NYC that weekend to shop as it was Thanksgiving weekend. At the site of the destruction now labeled Ground Zero, multitudes of people surrounded the site, waiting for their chance to look at the area. We were able to talk, pray and encourage many during this sorrowful time, as well as minister to the homeless and downtrodden we found there.

Naturally we did a lot of walking all over the city. That is the first time I remember Pat complaining about pain in his left hip. A little arthritis, we thought. He took a few ibuprofens and was okay for a while. Although he said it still hurt when he walked, we really didn't think any more about it.

As the winter wore on, Pat started limping more from the pain in his hip. He went to the doctor, but no tests were made of his hip. Sounded like arthritis, they said. His doctor advised him to take more ibuprofen, which he did, but without much relief.

Though in pain, Pat and I organized a second outreach to NYC in the spring of 2002. This time our team was able to stay at the Bowery Mission in lower Manhattan. It was an opportunity of a lifetime. Because the mission was a shelter for the homeless as well as serving food three times a day, their doorway was always filled with very needy people. We were able to reach many of these beautiful but broken ones with the love of God, hot food and encouragement. Pat was out on the streets every day and climbed five flights of steps daily to reach his sleeping quarters, despite his pain worsening.

Within weeks of returning from that trip, Pat's pain became even more severe. We knew arthritis usually didn't progress that fast. We begged his doctor for tests and finally Pat had a standard X-ray. Strange lesions were found but the X-ray was inconclusive. The doctor ordered an MRI but we had to wait one month to have that done. Finally, the results of the MRI came back. It revealed *multiple abnormalities in his pelvis and lesions on the top of his femur bones.* We didn't know what that meant. We were confused but knew our mighty God was in control. He would take care of us. We prayed and waited. The doctors did more examinations and blood tests to see what the diagnosis could be. We were sure it wasn't anything serious. We had been married only a little over a year and had so many great plans for the future.

June 10, 2002 was the day of Pat's diagnosis. The doctor did not tell us it was cancer; he said it was *multiple myeloma*, and left the room. We didn't know what that meant, but we knew Pat needed treatment right away. We knew that no matter what, our God would be with us and help us get through whatever we would be facing.

I went to the library after our strange meeting with the doctor to find out more about the disease we were dealing with. This disease 'multiple myeloma', was actually cancer of the bone marrow. The chances of contracting it are 1 in a 100. I was in shock as I read the prognosis from a library article:

The life expectancy of someone who had late stage multiple myeloma, [which Pat had], was one and one-half to three years.

I wanted to faint on the spot.

This must be a wrong diagnosis! This cannot possibly be true, I thought. No, it can't, it can't, it cannot be true! Neither one of us had realized how terribly serious this disease was.

I went home and fell on my knees, crying out to the Living God for a miracle and Pat's life. I had to tell Pat what I had discovered, then together we joined forces in prayer and intercession for his very life. We had hope, great hope in fact. We had seen how God had delivered us both in the past and how God had given Pat grace to be alive this long. We knew that our lives were only on loan from Heaven.

We would have to trust God 100% with our future. Pat was not moved by the diagnosis even though his pain increased. He knew God would be faithful, no matter what. We had to believe God for a miracle. There was no other option.

Within days, Pat was admitted into the hospital and stayed there for weeks at a time, fighting one infection after the other. He lost weight quickly and contracted a severe blood clot in his leg. Things were not looking very good, to say the least.

His cancer was already very advanced and, they told me, possibly untreatable. His one hope was a bone marrow transplant, which *might* work, *if* he was a candidate and *if* the doctors could keep him alive that long. He might have to wait one full year to get a transplant as he was in the Veterans Administration (VA) system. Meanwhile, the doctors began aggressive chemotherapy to keep the cancer at bay for as long as possible. Time was growing short; it didn't look good. No, not good at all.

Our emotions vacillated from extreme highs to lows and then back again! We both knew in our hearts that we trusted God and what His Word said. Jesus said, *"The thief [devil] comes only to steal and kill and destroy, but I [Jesus] have come that they may have life and have it to the full"* (John 10:10).

We knew that God didn't put this disease on Pat. We live in a fallen, broken world. Sin has brought a curse on the entire human race in which we live including sickness, pain, disease and ultimately death. However, Jesus atoned not only for our sins, but for our sicknesses and diseases as well on the cross of Calvary. Isaiah 53:4-5 says, *"Surely He [Jesus] has borne our grief and carried our sorrows; yet we esteemed Him stricken, smitten by God and afflicted. But He was wounded for our transgressions, He was bruised for our iniquities; the chastisement for our peace was upon Him, and by His stripes we are healed."* We were going to keep believing for a miracle and there was going to be no other option for us.

We both had strong confidence in God's Word and meditated on it every day of our journey. We wrote down scriptures, prayed over them and both grew much stronger in our faith. We didn't live in despair, but instead lived in peace, joy and great hope. Though our emotions went up and down, we had decided long ago that we would not live by our feelings or even what the circumstances looked like though they were often horrendous. Instead we were going to live 100% by God's Word. The Bible says, *"We live by faith, not by sight"* (2 Corinthians 5:7). We chose to live by faith.

Pat and I prayed together daily, even when he was in the hospital and we had to pray over the phone. We asked our Heavenly Father to deliver Pat and give him life. Here are a few excerpts from my journal at this time:

May 17, 2002

Pat is weak in body but strong in spirit. I today felt weak in both. I felt so strong yesterday then later today I feel sad, moody, mad and fearful. I woke up from not sleeping well at all but I know God will give me some encouragement.

God did give me encouragement as I opened my Bible, I read:

Isaiah 49:23b *"...those who hope in Me will not be disappointed."*

Isaiah 41:9b-10 *"...You are my servant; I have chosen you and have not rejected you. So do not fear, for I am with you; I will uphold you with my righteous right hand."*

Isaiah 43:1-5 *"But now, this is what the Lord says, He who created you, O Jacob, He who formed you O Israel: Fear not, for I have redeemed you; I have called you by name, you are Mine. When you pass through the waters, I will be with you; and when you pass through the rivers, they will not sweep over you. When you walk through the fire, you will not be burned; the flames will not set you ablaze. For I am the Lord, your God, the Holy One of Israel, your Savior;...Since you are precious and honored in my sight, and because I love you, I will give men in exchange for your life. Do not be afraid for I am with you..."*

Countless other encouraging scriptures were also written down in my journal.

By the hand and grace of God and after one year of intense rounds of chemotherapy and radiation, Pat finally qualified for his bone marrow transplant. The VA arranged for Pat and me to fly to Nashville, TN, in June, 2003 to the VA hospital for his transplant. Pat was to have an *autologous transplant*, which means *all* bone marrow from your body is removed and then purified as much as possible. Next, you are given incredibly high doses of chemotherapy, almost lethal, to hopefully kill every cancer cell in your body. The cleansed bone marrow is then infused back into your body.

This procedure can be very risky as one literally has no immune system at all for about three days and even the slightest germ could cause death. This procedure, however, is safer than receiving bone marrow from a donor as there is a large chance of rejection and an even higher risk of death from that.

Because of Pat's weakened state to begin with, Pat struggled greatly with his transplant. At one point, he was seconds from death. I was at his beside, but he was not responding to any stimuli. I called the nurse and within seconds, seven doctors were by his bedside trying everything they could. I could not bear to watch. I left the room crying out to God for a divine intervention. I called my nurse friend, Diane, who understood the medical problems, and she encouraged me to keep believing God's promises no matter what it looked like at the moment. God showed Himself so faithful once again and rescued Pat from the very brink of death.

A few weeks later, Pat was released from the hospital; he was recovering very slowly. We were to receive the report from his doctor four weeks after the transplant to see if his transplant was completely successful or not. If no cancer cells were found in his bone marrow, that would be a good indication that it had been successful. Pat and I were on edge and couldn't wait to get the results.

Soon, we met with his oncologist, Dr. V, (as she was nicknamed due to her extremely long last name). Dr. V tried to remain very positive during our meeting; she said, "Pat's bone marrow has *fewer* cancer cells now, but still shows a small percentage of cancer cells."

We could not really comprehend this; we were stunned. The transplant had been only marginally successful. Cancer was still in his body, meaning that it could easily become full blown again at any time. There was no other treatment available for Pat at this time. His body would not be able to withstand any other treatment for six months to one year. We wondered if he would even be able to live that long. The doctor had no way of knowing how long the transplant would ward off the cancer, so we had no way of knowing what kind of time frame we were dealing with. We had God and we had each other; we determined to hold on tight for dear life!

Though we knew cancer still lingered in Pat's body, I watched Pat grow stronger every day. His blood counts kept improving and his color and strength were gradually returning to him. We were so full of joy and praised God for his renewed life and energy.

At this point Pat had been confined to a wheelchair for one year due an unsuccessful surgery on his hip and leg a year earlier. The doctors told him he would need a total hip replacement now if he was ever to walk again, which seemed very doubtful. He would also need to be almost totally cancer free and very much recovered before he could endure such a large operation. The operation would involve a completely new hip and a rod to replace his deteriorated bone in his femur. The rod would extend from his hip to within two inches of his knee cap. It was called a *mega hip replacement* and was not usually performed. We prayed and stormed the gates of heaven with our families and friends. It seemed half the world was praying for us and we were so grateful. The VA did not have the capabilities or doctors to do this type of surgery.

However, by this time, we had learned to trust God and see Him make a way for us where there was no way. Sure enough, while we were in Nashville at a local hotel, awaiting Pat's bone marrow transplant, we had breakfast with a man who was having extensive surgeries from one of the best orthopedic oncologists in the country. We eagerly got his name and contact information—just in case.

The doctor was on staff at the Vanderbilt University Medical Center. It just so happened that the VA and Vanderbilt Hospital worked together at that time and shared doctors. (That is no longer the case.) In fact, the two hospitals were adjoined to each other by a bridge. That meant Pat might be able to get this famous surgeon to perform his hip surgery and it would be paid for by the VA.

Though I was so thankful of the prospects that Pat might walk again, I was emotionally and physically at my end. Eighteen months of intense ups and downs had left me completely drained. God had to pick me up or else. Here's what I wrote just before Pat's hip replacement:

October 2003

I have none, absolutely none, none, none of my strength or even will power right now. I don't have anything. I am so weak. I cling and hold onto the Word of God. *"I would have lost heart unless I had believed that I would see the goodness of the Lord in the land of the living. Wait on the Lord; be of good courage and He shall strengthen your heart; wait, I say, on the Lord!" (Psalm 27:13-14.)*

Those were words of strength and courage to me at that very moment. I knew David the shepherd boy had penned those words when his heart was failing thousands of years ago. That is the same David who slew the giant and became the great king of Israel. I had to believe that God would strengthen me the same way.

I also wrote a song at this time that never fully materialized but I will include it here as a poem on the state of my heart:

When this life has taken its toll
And I don't want to try anymore
When my head begins to roll
What in life's worth living for?
When my heart is empty and the world cold
When I can't make sense of ups and downs
When I'm weary and feeling old
When sickness, pain and troubles come

What in this life's worth living for?
What in this life's worth living for?
I remember a promise of long ago God said,
"Trust Me, child when you're feeling low"
He gave to me this precious seed,
"You'll dance with Me on streets of gold"
You asked Me to forgive your sins
Though heartaches come and you don't win
You trusted God to set you free
So now you're Mine eternally

Yes, I knew that was true. I do not live for this life. This life is not my own. It's God's, all the way. Good or bad, I live for Him. *"So far as the law is concerned, however I am dead- killed by the law itself, in order that I might live for God. I have been put to death with Christ on His cross, so that it is no longer I who live, but it is Christ who lives in me. This life that I live now, I live by faith in the Son of God, who loved me and gave His life for me"* (Galatians 2:19-20).

The great news was that after specially arranged meetings with all the doctors involved, Pat was able to have the famous surgeon and team from Vanderbilt perform his delicate and risky hip replacement; this happened incredibly only four months after his bone marrow transplant! Though Pat's upper femur and hip bone had been terribly eaten away by the cancer, the surgery was a 100% success. That was no small miracle to be sure. Our joy was exploding and how we praised the Lord!

By January, 2004, we were seeing miracle after miracle. We eagerly awaited tests from the doctor about the cancer as the reports were so negative in the past, but Pat was feeling so good. We knew the transplant did not remove all the cancer, but on April 4, 2004 we got the amazing news: no more cancer could be detected in his blood at all. Everything was clear! Pat had no multiple myeloma. This does not happen. I was overwhelmed and cried tears of joy. Pat was thrilled and though he didn't cry, he knew he was healed. We thanked the Lord and sang songs of praise to our wonderful God and Healer!

We saw Pat's primary care doctors and nurses shortly after we received this good report and they hugged and congratulated Pat on this wonderful news with tears streaming down their cheeks. Pat was also starting to walk again—with just a cane. What a miracle! We could walk and hold hands together again, just like when we fell in love. We were so excited that we decided to take an eight-day trip to Maui, Hawaii, to celebrate God's goodness and Pat's restored life. We felt like we were the most blessed couple in the entire world. How we both appreciated life and every single breath we took!

Oh yes, I forgot to mention that Pat felt so well that he was able to re-enroll in Bible school. He was very determined to complete his training and become a pastor. That was his dream.

During Pat's intense treatments, he had been put on 1800-2000 mg. of oxycotin daily to ease his pain, which is an extremely high dosage of the very strong, addictive narcotic. However, Pat wanted to get off all of his pain medications. The doctors were very leery because it was hardly ever done and could be very dangerous as Pat could experience severe withdrawal symptoms. Still, Pat insisted.

If you are in the medical field, you might think that the dosage is a misprint, but I assure you, it is not. The doctor told us that that dose could literally kill a horse, however, because of Pat's heavy drug use in the past, he had a very high tolerance for narcotics. He was taking one of the highest doses possible. Finally, the doctor agreed to give Pat a schedule that would allow him to slowly withdraw from all the narcotics. It took five months and though he did experience some withdrawal symptoms, Pat diligently persisted. By late spring, he was totally free of all narcotics. This was unheard of. The doctors shook their heads in amazement and disbelief, while we rejoiced. We knew God, our heavenly Father, had delivered Pat once again. Our whole lives lay ahead of us now and we knew it would be good. God was surely with us!

Life was good. Pat was in school again, and we were ministering at the Urban Center and also on staff at an inner city church. We were fulfilling our mutual dream of reaching out to the lost and broken. Our marriage was strong and our mini-battles had only helped us to draw so much closer to God and to each other.

Then around September 2004, I began noticing a disturbing gaze in Pat's eyes which concerned me. It reminded me of the look of illness, like children have when they get the flu. Instead of clearing up, his eyes appeared worse each day. I could tell something was definitely wrong. His body started to ache again. We both dreaded going to the doctor, but there was no choice. After extensive tests, the diagnosis came back: the cancer had returned and was growing rapidly. We prayed and believed God for another miracle. There were some new drugs available and Pat was able to take them for a while, but when there was no improvement, he would try a different one.

Pat continued in Bible school and in April 2005, he realized his dream. He marched down the aisle of the auditorium to receive his diploma. The guest speaker for the graduation was the TV evangelist, Pat Robertson. When Patrick walked up on stage, the entire audience of over 1,000 people leapt to their feet and gave him a standing ovation! Pat Robertson didn't know what to make of all the ruckus and turned to ask the president of the school why everyone was standing. He had no idea about Pat or how dearly loved Pat was by all the students and faculty at the school and that they had prayed for him for years. I was so very proud of my husband that day, I thought my chest would pop. I could not hold back my tears of joy knowing how much he had studied and worked through many months - even years of intense pain and treatments. Now, Pat had finally received his diploma.

Shortly thereafter, Pat was credentialed as a licensed minister with Elim Fellowship, Lima, NY. We were both so happy and gave God all the glory and praise. We knew God would continue to make a way. We kept clinging to this verse for Pat's life: *"I will not die but live and declare the works of the Lord"* (Psalm 118:17). I even wrote a song from that verse; we sang it almost every day to encourage ourselves in God's Word.

We didn't know for sure what the future held as Pat seemed to be fighting the demon of cancer more every day. We needed to take a break from all the intensity of school and his illness, plus we wanted to celebrate his graduation so we flew to San Francisco for two weeks and also toured Yosemite National Park and many other beautiful spots. Though Pat was growing weaker, he still enjoyed the trip immensely. We both appreciated his life and this time God had given us together. However, there were two very frightening episodes during the trip that could have ended in disaster.

The first episode happened as we were driving from San Francisco to Yosemite National Park; suddenly Pat started to experience intense breathing problems. It sounded as if he was on the verge of pneumonia and I knew that it could easily cause death if he wasn't treated quickly due to his weakened condition. I immediately called our church and everyone prayed fervently for Pat's life. Within hours, his breathing cleared up and we went onto Yosemite and actually camped in the park. Another answer to prayer!

However, during the third night there, a severe rattling started in Pat's chest. I could hear fluid gurgling in his lungs and as I reached out and touched his forehead, I could feel he was burning up with fever. Worst of all, we were in the middle of nowhere! I cried out to God to intervene for us and heal Pat and to even let us enjoy the rest of the trip! I desperately called a friend to pray. I knew if Pat didn't improve within a few hours, he would have to be ambulanced or flown out to the nearest hospital. It was another very critical situation. Looking back in the natural, I should have called 911 instantly, but by now, we had been in and out of emergency rooms more than fifty times and we just couldn't bear to think about it again. Thankfully by morning, all Pat's breathing problems were completely gone! We knew it was due to the mighty prayers of all our friends and we continued with joy on the rest of our trip, just as I had prayed!

The following months became increasingly difficult for Pat. His body was not able to withstand the onslaught of the cancer. The doctors could only give him low doses of chemotherapy due to his deteriorating health. Finally we heard of a new experimental drug and Pat qualified to try it. It was our last hope, but we always had God no matter what would happen.

Pat started the dosage and we were sure he would be cured. However, within two weeks, his face became spotted, red and blotchy. We returned to the doctor only to discover that he was having a severe allergic reaction to the medicine and he had to discontinue it immediately. We were overwhelmed with sadness. How could this possibly be? There were no other treatments available. Nothing. Well, nothing here in the United States anyway...

Chapter 19

Supernatural Intervention

We had to take action fast. With no more treatment options left, Pat would only live a few more months and endure great pain. I searched the internet for alternative treatments outside of the US. After much research and prayer, we decided to attempt alternative treatment at Oasis Cancer Hospital, a Christian-based hospital in Tijuana, Mexico. The treatment plan called for three intense intervals of treatment spaced months apart. After the first round of treatment, Pat definitely improved and a large tumor on his chest that would not respond to any other treatment completely disappeared within two months! We were so encouraged. As always, we kept believing God for Pat's complete healing. This hospital was our last hope other than divine intervention, but we were going to give it all we had.

Unfortunately, Pat did not fare well at all during the next two treatments at Oasis Hospital but instead grew steadily worse. After our third trip, we realized from Pat's poor blood tests that Oasis Hospital had no more plan of treatment available for Pat. His blood counts, including his red, white and platelet cells continued to plummet which meant more emergency room visits, transfusions and endless prayer. It was now August, 2006 and Pat's depleted body could not tolerate any more treatment for the cancer whatsoever. The only thing he had was extremely high doses of medication to ease his pain.

We had one last scare and yet a great miracle too. It was September, 2006. For days, I could see Pat regressing. I was attempting to feed him because he had stopped eating on his own. He was starting to become unresponsive so I rushed him to the VA hospital again, 80 miles away, where he was immediately ushered into ICU.

Pat's room became a flurry of activity, IVs, blood draws, X-rays and doctor visits. After receiving four units of blood plus platelets, I thought Pat would be doing much better and he actually was a little better for a short time. But all his blood counts fell again rapidly, meaning he was not making any new blood cells or, basically, sustaining life. The next day, more transfusions. Again, his counts improved but quickly dipped to near fatal levels. His blood counts at this time were: white blood cells were .3, hemoglobin was 4.8, platelets were 13. If you understand medical terms, you realize the extreme urgency of the situation. I called Pat's mother from out of town and explained his condition. Within a few hours she rushed in to see her son, not knowing if this would be the last time she would see him alive.

Pat continued to hold on to a sliver of life. He couldn't talk and to make matters worse, he was running a temperature. His stomach started swelling also- a real sign of infection. The doctors informed us that his bone marrow had now reached the point where it could not manufacture any more new blood cells. I understood all too well what that meant. Unless God intervened in hours or perhaps even minutes, Pat would be in heaven very soon.

A nurse approached me in the hall. She knew Pat's condition and saw my pain. She paused, rubbed my shoulder and, with a look of sadness in her eyes, told me how very sorry she was. She knew my husband was dying and was trying to comfort me. I shook my head, meaning thanks, but inwardly I was crying out, *No God, no, no no! Rescue my husband. He needs a miracle right this very moment. O God, deliver us!*

Shortly all the pastors from our church arrived; they anointed Pat with oil and prayed fervently for him. They loved Pat deeply and understood that without a miracle their good friend and my beloved husband was going to be with Jesus very, very soon. There is no doubt in my mind that God heard all our prayers. There is no other answer that can explain the fact that miraculously, one week later *Pat triumphantly walked out of that hospital* without even the aid of a walker!

His bone marrow *did* start making red blood cells again and Pat looked healthier than he had looked in the last year! This is what I wrote in my journal at that time:

"The devil was *defeated* when we walked out of those hospital doors yesterday. *It felt so good,* as we could have been going to a *funeral* and Pat would have been the main attraction!"

Oh how we both rejoiced and praised our mighty God. Pat always referred to God as the *Living God* and I never felt God was more living and working in our lives than that glorious day as we literally skipped out of those hospital doors. Halleluia!

Only three days later, we were able to take a two-day camping trip in our little RV to a beautiful state park close to our home. We even celebrated our sixth anniversary there on September 24, 2006. Just to have my husband by my side *and alive* was a thrill and joy that I treasured deep within my soul. We knew that Pat was living on borrowed time and we would trust God for every single day He blessed us with. On the second evening camping, I felt God was speaking deep inside my heart. It was something I really didn't want to hear but I knew it was God's Spirit. This is what I heard: "Sandy, are you willing to release Pat totally to Me, even if I want to take him home?" Being overwhelmed with five years of Pat's debilitating disease, I was at the end of my natural strength. I knew that I needed to release Pat and his life or death to God once and for all. Solemnly, I answered the Lord, "Yes, Lord, I will totally surrender him to You. He is Yours. Not my will, Lord, but Yours." These verses from Psalm 116: 1-11 really encouraged me at this time:

I love the Lord because He hears me; He listens to my prayers. He listens every time I call to Him. The danger of death was all around me; the horrors of the grave closed in on me; I was filled with fear and anxiety. Then I called to the Lord, "I beg you, Lord, save me!" The Lord is merciful and good; our God is compassionate. The Lord protects the helpless; when I was in danger, He saved me. Be confident my heart, because the Lord has been good to me. The Lord saved me from death; He stopped my tears and kept me from defeat. And so I walk in the presence of the Lord in the world of the living. I kept on believing even when I said, "I am completely crushed," even when I was afraid and said, "No one can be trusted." (Good News)

Yes, though our souls were crushed beyond measure, we would be confident in the Lord. He had always been, was and would always be good to us. We would keep on believing—period.

Though Pat was still having tremendous struggles and pain, I clearly remember a special date we had in October. Pat wined and dined me at Red Lobster, just like when we were falling in love. He was in an unusually humorous mood that night, joking and making me giggle and we had a simply beautiful and romantic evening together. I wrote in my journal, "I was so happy; I know Pat loves me so much." Yes, he did.

Before we knew it, Thanksgiving was upon us, and Pat and I decided to visit his family three hours away in Binghamton, NY. It was wonderful to be around his mom, sisters, brother and extended family and being able to feel normal, if even just for a few days.

Our visit was cut short however when Pat started having much difficulty breathing. We knew it was a sign that his red blood cells weren't making enough oxygen. We rushed home and then on to the hospital for more transfusions. The next few months were very, very troublesome for both of us. Pat would be fairly well for one or two weeks and then would need to be rushed back to the emergency room for more transfusions. His pain was growing increasingly worse and by this point he could hardly walk at all. The Lord continued to encourage us both with many scriptures that gave us great strength when we had *absolutely none* of our own. We needed to lean on the Lord with everything within us!

We were not able to travel at Christmas, but his three daughters and grandchildren as well as my son and family from Buffalo were able to be with us at our home. I'll never forget that precious Christmas Eve. Pat was hurting, but didn't complain. He was glad to have his children and loved ones around him and we were elated that we all could spend this special season with Pat.

New Year's Eve was just as special that December in 2006. Pat's best friend, Hector and his wife Bernadette came over for a steak dinner. We ate, laughed, talked and even worshipped the Lord as I played my guitar. Pat grabbed the tambourine, slowly hobbled up and danced before the Lord with any little bit of strength his feeble body could muster up, just like he used to do in church. He danced and twirled around one minute or less on his thin, scraggly legs, but I believe in God's eye that that minute was equal to an eternity. I know God must have had a big smile on His face. We felt God's hand of pleasure on all of us that evening. We went to bed full of joy and thankfulness for a new year to just be *alive*. What a night to remember.

Days passed and Pat was in and out of the hospital two more times. His weight was dropping fast and we both knew we had to have a miracle or else. I wrote in my journal: "We are broken and desperate, yet we don't give up."

During his last hospital stay, the doctors told Pat there was nothing more they could do for him and that it was best for him to go home and be with family. His kidneys were failing due to the cancer. All his organs were now severely affected. If we looked at the circumstances, they looked terribly frightening, but we kept our eyes and heart set on God's Holy Word alone. I suppose I'm an eternal optimist as I wrote in my journal, "Well, Pat's bad, but not as bad as Lazarus!" (Lazarus was a friend of Jesus who died and Jesus raised him from the dead three days later – see John 11:1-44.) "We *more* than *only believe*, we are expecting. We are pregnant with God's promises. We have the Living Seed in us. It is *alive* in us when nothing much else is."

Pat came home a few days later. Many of his friends and family gathered around him. Our time together was very precious. My nephew Rog and his wife Karen called me the day he came home and wanted to come visit us the following weekend. I was so excited that they could come, but I begged them to come sooner. I knew time was of the essence. Karen said it looked totally impossible due to her work schedule, but she would try. She had dozens of meetings lined up, however, as soon as she started looking for airline tickets, all her meetings were miraculously cancelled and she had an open schedule. Both Rog and Karen were able to get off work and be in Rochester with us within just a few days. How glad I was to see them. Pat was able to visit and talk with them for a while before he needed to go to bed. It was so comforting and reassuring to have my family around.

Later, Pat and I gently kissed goodnight as we snuggled up to sleep that evening. About 1:30 AM, Pat woke up, gasping for air. He was not able to get his breath no matter how high I turned up his oxygen supply. I quickly dialed 911 and then called my nephew and wife downstairs to come and pray with us. Within minutes the ambulance arrived and we all sped to a local hospital in the middle of a blinding snow storm, crying out to God for deliverance. Immediately Pat was rushed into emergency and diagnosed with severe pneumonia. It was strange that he had no symptoms just hours before, but now no matter what the doctors tried, Pat still could barely breathe. Morphine was administered to calm his breathing.

The doctors told me that Pat only had a few hours to live, however I already knew that in my heart. Yet, instead of panic and fear, I felt heavy waves of God's amazing grace and peace surround me. I could almost reach out and touch it. In fact, it was so strong that I thought maybe there was something wrong with me for not feeling more upset. I called our pastor, friends and family and shortly Pat was surrounded by at least fifteen people who loved him dearly. I spent some quiet moments just hugging and holding him and released him once and for all into God's hands. I told Pat it was okay now to go home to live with his Savior forever and ever. We kissed tenderly. Pat told me he loved me with the little breath he had left.

The minutes dragged on with every labored breath. Minutes turned into hours. My nephew Rog started reading Revelation 21 over Pat as I held him tightly by my side. Revelation 21 is the description of heaven and the place where Pat was about to pass into. I remember hearing these comforting words:

"He will wipe away all tears from their eyes. There will be no more death, no more grief or crying or pain. The old things have disappeared... The wall was made of jasper, and the city itself was made of pure gold, as clear as glass. The foundation stones of the city wall were adorned with all kinds of precious stones. The first foundation stone was jasper, the second sapphire, the third agate, the fourth emerald, the fifth onyx, the sixth carnelian, the seventh yellow quartz, the eighth beryl, the ninth topaz, the tenth chalcedony, the eleventh turquoise, the twelfth amethyst. The twelve gates were twelve pearls; the gate was made from a single pearl. The street of the city was of pure gold, transparent as glass.

I did not see a temple in the city because the temple is the Lord God Almighty and the Lamb. The city has no need of the sun or the moon to shine on it, because the glory of God shines on it, and the Lamb is its lamp." (Revelation 21:4, 18-23) (Good News.)

Pat was very much at peace and I believe very eager to receive his heavenly reward. The earth had no more hold on him and Jesus was waiting to show Pat his brand new home. At 7:36 AM, January 20, 2007, Pat stepped from this earthly life into the arms of his loving Savior, Jesus, the Lamb of God. We knew now he would be free from the terrible pain that racked his body and he would live forever in a new world of total joy being in the very presence of the Creator Himself.

Of course, I was deeply saddened, yet I knew and believed that this was the designated time for Pat's new life in heaven to begin and his life on earth to come to a close. I had surrendered Pat to the Lord and now I relinquished my entire being to my Creator. He would have to be my husband now and take care of me. Yes, Jesus was my everything and all I had.

Funeral arrangements were made quickly. We decided to hold the service at our alma mater, the chapel at Elim Bible Institute. We didn't think our church would be able to hold all the people that would attend and we were right. The chapel at Elim was packed with hundreds of people that day. Both of our families were there and that was so comforting to me. I continuously felt God's hand of comfort, love and grace upon me and I knew I was getting through all this by His power and strength alone. Pat's best friends and pastor spoke. We worshipped God, knowing Pat was now rejoicing and out of his excruciating pain. Pat truly was dancing with Jesus now.

One wonderful, yet bittersweet moment touched my heart deeply at the funeral. Though Pat had graduated from the Bible school, somehow he lacked one class to actually receive his official diploma. When Pat was handed his diploma at graduation, there was a card inside saying, "Almost There" instead of his diploma. He had planned on finishing that course but was unable to due to his failing health.

The president of the Bible School and Pat's friend, Rev. Jeff Clark, was one of the speakers at the funeral. In the middle of his eulogy, he turned to me, walked down the steps from the altar, and presented me with Pat's full diploma, posthumously. I was stunned, happy and yet sorrowful at the same time. Tears tumbled down my cheeks. I still cherish that diploma many years later.

My visitors left just days following the funeral and I was left alone. I had the entire house to myself—no pets, no roommate, just God and me. Fortunately, Judy and Barbara, two dear friends from St. Louis, MO, my hometown, came to visit me two weeks after the funeral. They were a great comfort to me. There was only one problem. I didn't want them to ever go home!

Days and weeks passed. I was sick and getting more ill by the day. It started with a severe cold on the day of the funeral. No matter what I did, I only recovered for a few days at best. I realize now that the stress of the last few years had finally hit me. I had no immune system to fight off this bug. I tried many immune system boosters which only worked for short periods of time. My emotions started running wild. Here is an entry I wrote in my journal during those first trying days:

Dear Father God, I am so mixed up right now. Up and down, down and up, sad, hurting, hurting deeply, mourning, grieving, trying to get by with You. My life has changed so drastically. It is so quiet around here, too quiet. I miss Pat so so much, I can't even tell You, Lord. He was my right arm, my strength, my joy, however, all those things are to be found in You. You really are all those things. I know somehow You and I will make it through. Somehow, You will carry me. I am exhausted, tired, sad and mixed up. Don't have many answers, just want You! There will never be another man like Pat. He was my bosom buddy. He was my soul-mate. Lord, nothing makes sense right now! How will I go on? How, O how will I cope without the love of my life? Wouldn't it have been easier just to have never met him? O God, why have you forsaken me?

Love, Your daughter, Sandy

This is God's response to my heart a few moments after I wrote the above:

Dear daughter Sandy,

Don't worry, My precious daughter, I haven't forsaken you, not even for one moment. You are still the twinkle in My eye and I delight in you. I am so sorry to see you suffering, but remember I also watched My Son, Jesus suffer, even unto death. I hold you in the palm of My hand. I am comforting you. I am your all in all, your strength, your joy, your NEW hope, your NEW life, your NEW purpose. I haven't left you for one second. You and I go way back, don't we? You have walked some very difficult roads with Me and haven't I gotten you through victoriously through every single one?

Right now, all seems unbearable and impossible, but with Me you will begin to see My plan. My plans for you are good, to give you a hope and a future. You WILL dance again. You WILL sing again. You WILL love again and you WILL fulfill every purpose I have put you on earth to complete. You ARE My precious daughter and I won't forget you! Rest, be still and know that I AM GOD. I AM your true love. I AM your all in all. I AM all and everything you need. Pat could never meet all those needs. Let ME meet every single, single, single need of yours right now. You WILL be OK my darling. I love you—even more than Pat ever could.

Love,

Your Father God

God's Word comforted me greatly during these early days. I hung on His Word in my heart but also to His written Word in Revelation 21 and 22 where there is penned a glorious description of heaven. What a glorious day that will be when we meet our Savior face to face! I also read First Corinthians 15 over and over, especially where it says that we will put off this corruptible body and put on incorruption and I couldn't wait.

I also learned a few other things as time went by: I worshipped the Lord with my guitar or with praise CDs every single day for an hour or more. I wanted to be in God's presence as much as I possibly could. I also would talk a lot about my husband, the funeral, etc. to anyone who would listen. I cried and cried and just let it all out. I certainly did not disguise my feelings, but told God exactly how I felt every day. I made a list of my favorite scriptures and would say them out loud. They were confessions of how I wanted to feel, not how I was feeling at the moment. I called my relatives in St. Louis and reminisced about my dear husband. I asked people to pray for me whenever possible.

Little by little, if ever so gently, I did start hearing God's voice again. Actually, that is how this book came to be. Sometime after Pat's death, I was standing in another room with the TV blaring when I heard a voice from the TV say, "You should write a book." I had been thinking of that very thing for quite a while and I knew instantly when I heard that voice that it really was God speaking to me to just do it! I told God out loud, "O Lord, I know that was You. Okay, okay, yes, I will. I don't know how, but I will!"

About the same time, the Lord gave me a song to express my feelings – feelings of being ripped apart inside yet clinging on to my hope in Christ. Here are the words:

1.

I sit here contemplating this journey that I'm on
I tell you, Lord, I don't understand; it seems so long, so hard
I ask the question why O Lord, things turned out this way
It's hard to hear Your voice now though I ask You night and day
CHORUS
No, I won't give up when the day turns dark and the pain cuts
deep down inside my heart
Yes, one day Lord I will understand, but for now I take hope and
take my stand
You are my God faithful and true. You turn grief to joy;
You make my life new
You wipe away the teardrops that fall
You walk beside me; You answer my call

2.

The answers that I seek Lord, seem like a fading mist
Won't You give a reason why; O God how I wish
But now I must just trust in You though doubts and fears are
great
Your love for me is greater still; You won't leave me as I wait
CHORUS

3.
The stinging tears keep coming; I feel so lost, so sad
My life feels like it's over. Will I again be glad
I feel like I've been cut in two; so much is gone from me
But I will chose to live again, to be all that I can be
CHORUS

Yes, I had to *choose* life and to live life to the fullest as God had ordained. Nothing in me wanted that at all, but I knew that was God's plan for me and I chose by faith to go ahead through the uncharted waters of the future, but not alone, I was with Him. I also hung onto to my life verse; this was the verse God planted in my heart years ago when I first found the Lord and I still cherish it today with all my heart:

"*Do not remember the former things, nor consider the things of old. Behold I will do a new thing, now it shall spring forth; shall you not know it? I will even make a road in the wilderness and rivers in the desert.*" (Isaiah 43:18-19.)

A few months after Pat's death, I found a grief support group through a local church. It was a 13-week course called 'Griefshare'. It was a lifeline to me and I found that many others struggled as deeply or even deeper than I did. This course, which I actually took twice, is a national program and available in most major cities in the US. Check out griefshare.org for more information or to sign up for their daily word of encouragement. I highly recommend it. I knew deep down God would restore me one day. I was just wishing He would hurry up.

Though a part of me seemed to be healing at first, as time went by, another wave of grief, shock and desperation developed only to grow deeper and darker than ever. I started getting very angry. I really didn't know who to be angry with. I was actually angry at Pat for leaving me (how dare he!), angry at myself for somehow not finding a cure for Pat, angry at the devil who had no authority over Pat and me, but mostly I turned my anger toward God.

I didn't know who to yell at, so I let all my anger out on Him. I told Him the good, the bad and the ugly. I knew God totally understood; and after my anger subsided, I realized I could not stay angry with God, nor did I want to. An old friend of mine did that, and she actually drew away from God. I did not want that ever to happen to me. I knew God held everything in His hands, especially life and death. He was God and I surely was not and no matter how much I kicked and screamed, He had His own reason for allowing my husband to die at age fifty-five. I had to trust Him. I sincerely repented of my anger toward God and asked Him to fill me with His peace and love instead.

I kept somewhat busy with friends, but I was on a *compassion leave* at my job, which meant I wasn't working. I really wanted to work and stay focused at this time, but I did not have a choice. My life seemed totally empty. I didn't want to live anymore. I *did not* want to take my life, I just wanted to be with Pat in heaven and forget about anything this world had to offer. Weeks turned into months and I was slipping into a deep depression. I remember crying for hours on my couch and feeling like I was going down into a bottomless pit. I started feeling afraid of what was happening to me. If I went any deeper into this deep, dark hole, I wasn't sure if there would be any way out. I realized I was starting to slip over the line and was starting to become mentally unstable. I had never been like this in my life before, not even after my divorce.

I have prayed about sharing the ending of my story, and the only thing I can come up with is to tell the absolute truth. I could sugarcoat it and make myself sound *so* spiritual, but I don't have all the answers as to why my grief was so intense, but all I know is—*it was*. Horrible, deep and extremely painful. That is just how I felt and it was getting worse by the minute. Here is another entry from my journal a few weeks later:

Why couldn't You have healed him, God? Why couldn't we go to the nations together? Why can't I hold Pat again? Why God? Why did You take him?

There was no answer. In the silence I cried, *Oh, God, what's happening to me?*

Weeks and months passed. Although I felt God drawing and comforting me, I also felt the enemy of my soul pulling me deeper into depression. Looking back over this time, I believe there was an intense battle for my very soul and perhaps my very life. One thing is for sure, the enemy of my soul, Satan himself, hated me, as he passionately hates you too. He would have loved to destroy all of me—my body, mind and soul. At times I felt like perhaps he was winning. I couldn't try anymore. People prayed, but I felt so isolated from life and friends. Even though I could put on a nice smile on the outside, it was only a mask. In truth, I was dying on the inside. Every day my burden got heavier and heavier.

One day I realized what I was feeling: I would feel a heavy blanket of doom, gloom and depression envelop my entire being. To make things worse, as I walked around, I could almost smell the spirit of death upon me. I felt as though Pat's diseased and decaying dead corpse was attached to my back and I was hauling it around with me everywhere I went. I know it's not a pretty picture, but that's exactly what it felt like. There is no way that I could function like that. I was too proud to tell anyone. After all, what would they think? I did tell friends I was grieving deeply, but they all assured me that this was just normal grief. I disagree. Somehow, I had crossed over a line.

I knew I could get medication from my doctor, but I hated the thought of getting addicted to any type of drugs. That, I prayed, would not be an option for me. I knew that somehow God would deliver me and get me out of this pit, but nothing seemed to be working. I was getting desperate. I arranged to have my grandkids over to visit often. I thought for sure when they were there that I would be fine, but even then I would be overcome with the worst dread and depression I had ever known. Something had to give. There had to be an answer, somewhere- somehow.

I prayed and sought the Lord as to what to do. I knew I had to take some action before it was too late. You may believe the following or not, but I have to be honest about how God truly delivered me. As background, I'd like to add that about three months after I became a follower of Jesus, I desired only more of Him and His Spirit. Whatever God had for me, I wanted. I had read in the Bible how He filled the early believers with His Holy Spirit, including speaking in unknown tongues and that it was for any believer— even today. This is not to say anyone is more holy or spiritual if he or she does receive this gift, but I wanted to receive this powerful gift of His Spirit. I sought God and simply asked Him to give me this gift many years ago and He did. Over the years, praying in tongues has been a great blessing to me and has enabled me to pray at length when I found I didn't have the words in English anymore.

So here I was, many years later in this huge battle. After prayer, I decided to bind the enemy every single time I felt this wave of horrible depression attack me. I would boldly say something to this effect with the all authority given to me and each believer, by Jesus Himself (see Matthew 16:19, 18:18-19; Mark 16:17-18): *"In the name of Jesus, I command the spirit of depression, oppression, sadness and extreme grief to leave me now! Every attack against me must stop now in Jesus' name. These spirits have no authority over me. I am free and full of God's love and peace right now!"* Then I would pray in tongues for extended periods as the Spirit of God led me.

At first, I felt no change, but within days I realized these attacks against me were of shorter and shorter duration. Instead of being overcome daily with these horrific episodes, the attacks would come only every other day and then slowly begin to decrease even more. I continued to bind these evil spirits and pray in tongues every single time I felt overwhelmed. I was persistent as I knew the enemy was going to be very persistent too. I knew I had to have the victory. Within one month, I was free and full of God's peace. I still had grief and sadness, but the deep depression and feeling of death that had been enveloping me was totally gone. God had delivered me by His power and Spirit. I praised and thanked Him for His goodness in setting me free. What a huge relief that was!

In all the many years of knowing my Savior, this was the first time ever I had been delivered by praying in tongues. According to the Bible, Jesus has given us many gifts of the Spirit; speaking in tongues in only one of the spiritual gifts. (See 1 Corinthians 12:1-11.) Jesus heals today as He did when He walked the earth in many different and sometimes unique ways. He chose to answer my cry for deliverance this way, this time. All I know is that I was free. Every once in a great while during the next year, the feeling of dread would again start to envelop me but I quickly bound the enemy and prayed in tongues again. Eventually, it never came back.

Life was starting to finally get a little better; I could see light now at the end of the tunnel, is even justs a tiny glimmer...

Note:

I love the Bride of Christ, His Church and everyone in it and I greatly desire to see unity in the Body. If your belief system is different from what you just read, please know I respect you as a fellow believer and I hope you can do the same. I do, however, ask you to search the scriptures for yourself. There is so much more God has for all of us – He gives good gifts to His children!

.

Though life was very hard, especially that first year, with God's help I was determined to go forward with my life. There was no way I could ever get my husband back. The only way to healing and health was to keep moving forward. And so I went.

Only three months after Pat's death, a friend invited me to go with her on a two-week mission outreach to the Ukraine. After prayer, I felt a moving in my spirit to go and so I said yes. The mission group I was going with had booked two separate trips, back to back. I was scheduled for the first trip with my airline tickets in hand; I was ready to go! However, about two weeks before my departure, I thought I was having a severe asthma attack, but the more inhalers I used, the worse I became. I was shaking like a leaf and didn't realize that I was also burning up with fever.

Finally, I decided I had to get help quick, so a friend rushed me to the ER. What I thought was asthma turned out to be pneumonia and I was immediately admitted to the hospital. I was shocked. I could hardly breathe and the treatments scarcely seemed to help. My trip was looming closer. How was I going to go to the Ukraine? My emotions were up and down. I knew God had a good future planned for me but because of my grief, I told the Lord it was just fine to take me home to be with Him and Patrick if He wanted. It would have been very easy to just give up. Somehow, the Spirit of God within me would not allow that.

I did pray in my weakness for God to intervene and many of my friends did too. Finally after five days, I was released from the hospital, but the first trip, the one that I was supposed to be on, had already left. I told the doctors I was planning now to go on the second trip instead and they thought I was just a little crazy! I knew however, God did plan for me to go and the devil himself was determined to do all he could to stop me. God answered my prayer in a mighty way. The travel agent was able to rebook my ticket without any fees and I did fly to the Ukraine with the second team only eight days after my release from the hospital.

Though I still cried at times and fought depression during the trip, seeing others so much worse off than myself in a foreign land helped bring me back to reality. It was on that trip that God endued me with His supernatural compassion like never before. I was on the prayer team for large women's conferences there. As the women would come forward for prayer, I would weep with them from the bottom of my heart as they told me stories of their troubled and seemingly hopeless lives. God used me not only in spite of my extreme brokenness, but *because* of my extreme brokenness. He certainly does use the foolish things of the world to confound the wise! (1 Corinthians 1:27). By the way, I felt great the entire trip, with lots of strength and energy; that was certainly a God thing. I am so glad God enabled me to go on that trip and I will never forget those amazing two weeks.

Slowly my life started taking form again. I joined with a pastor in Rochester, NY, Rev. Gary Hamm, and helped him establish a large outreach ministry of small Bible study groups and a training school throughout the inner city. I volunteered in a homeless ministry again and eventually founded an inner city ministry I named *Restoring the City Outreach Ministry*. I poured my heart out to the hurting and homeless as I could certainly relate to pain and loneliness. It was God's grace alone that did and always does inspire and empower me to do His work. I know I have no strength on my own. I am so thankful God allows me to go where others might fear to tread and share His delivering power and grace to the least and the lost. I cling to His grace alone.

The Lord also opened doors for me to start a *drop-in center* and weekly Bible study in a local homeless mission, St. Josephs' House of Hospitality, and serve in their shelter and other programs. Also, a street ministry to serve hot pizza, provide haircuts and God's Word to the needy and homeless was established in a small park every spring through fall. We had a wonderful time each Friday sharing God's love, food and clothing too. A great team took over that ministry, and it is still continuing as I write this.

For months after Pat's passing, I tried to find a widows' support group, but to no avail. I thought, *there has to be one somewhere.* As I was praying and crying out to the Lord about this one day, I heard the Lord speaking to my heart saying, "Sandy, you start one."

"Start one?" I said, "No way. I wouldn't even know where to begin!". However, God continued to nudge my broken heart and 17 months after Pat's death, I held my first support meeting for widowed, divorced and separated women called *Women of Restored Destinies* in my home. Though women came and went, many lives have been touched and comforted by God's grace through this ministry. These women have become very dear to my heart and together God healed our brokenness. I always told them that they helped heal me more than they would ever know, and I was so very thankful to each one of them. Though I now live in a new city, two years ago I started the same group here and again the healing continues in both the ladies and me.

I discovered through pioneering these various outreaches from the ground up and only being led by the Holy Spirit, that if we just say 'yes' to God, He will use our availability and will give us HIS ability. When we follow His guidance and walk by faith, God will do great things! It's not what we know but who we know—Jesus!

Two years after my husband passed away, I was able to go to Peru with my church family from Naples, NY, for two weeks to minister to the many needs of the poor. Only ten days later I was off to the Fiji Islands with *Youth With a Mission Mercy Ship* for a medical outreach for three weeks. We branched out all over the island of Vanua Levu and anchored in Nabowalu, a very poor but beautiful town. There, aboard the ship, the ophthalmologist and team removed cataracts from over 80 islanders; I conducted many eye exams and helped distribute over 700 pairs of prescription glasses with my team.

So many of the islanders were so thankful to be able to see again. People who had suffered from cataracts for 24 years actually cried after surgery when the bandages were removed and their vision was restored. Some grandmas and grandpas had never seen their grandchildren before. Imagine the joyous screams and hugs when they realized that though they had been blind for so many years, they could finally see their grandchildren for the first time!

Others in our group, including a doctor and a nursing team, held medical clinics in the villages while yet others provided clean water and water tanks plus housing construction to widows and orphans.

Everything was done free of charge. We only wanted to show them that there is a one true God who really cares for them. We were able to pray with hundreds of villagers and also tell them of our great Savior. I have to thank Jesus for all He allowed this team of 50 servants to accomplish.

Though the Peru and Fiji trips were extremely strenuous for me, they were very rewarding and again helped propel my life to live and serve God as He had called me to do in the past. Healing came more and more, although slowly, but yet it was coming.

Four years ago, I again had the awesome opportunity to return to Kenya as well as minister in Uganda for the first time. I really had been seeking the Lord about possibly living and ministering there long term. There is no better way to know than to go firsthand and see how God leads you while you are there, so off I went! I preached and sang songs God gave me in churches, went door to door in the slums to share Jesus, made new friends and gained two new beautiful spiritual daughters, Nelly and Daria.

Nelly is now reaching out on her own to pioneer her own ministry in Kenya!

Also in Kenya, I was driven deep into the *bush-bush*, as they say, to meet Mrs. Mwambe, a widow. Her mud hut had collapsed months before due to a cyclone. Now she and her tiny baby and four other children were forced to live in a tiny one-room hut built for animals to live in. I prayed, "Lord, we have to do something to help her!" By God's grace, on my return I was able to raise the funds for a new and much larger home for her and her children and that is where they now live. I thank the Lord for faithful people who give abundantly in such times of need.

I also hold very dear to my heart the three times I ministered in Kwale, Kenya, at the women's prison. WOW! I had visited many prisons here in the US, but this was surely quite a shock for me. Any children ages five and below had to live with the prisoners or the children would be homeless with no other place to live. Though the prison was clean, they did not have the funds to buy much of anything. There was no furniture at all. The ladies and children had no beds. They slept five to a room –in *very* hot rooms with hardly any circulation, on hard concrete floors. The prison did furnish thin foam mats.

The women had no toiletries available to them at all unless family members brought them in, which was very rare. Imagine, no soap, toothpaste, combs, underwear or anything else, just a change of your prison uniform weekly. The woman warden, a strong Christian lady, was brokenhearted for them and begged us to help in any way we could, and we were more than happy to oblige. My team and I made sure we brought as many goodies as we could carry to help them during the next two visits. We also brought diapers and clothes for the children as they too weren't provided with anything. In many third world countries, this is just how life is. There is no money to take care of anything above the very bare necessities of food and shelter.

I taught the ladies praise songs in Swahili and English and explained God's deep love for them. Every one of them responded, and we all shed a few tears when I departed for the last time. They were so hungry for visitors, attention and a giant dose of God's love. I will never forget these precious ladies.

I knew clearly during the trip that although I was having a great time ministering to the needy and hurting in Africa, God was calling me to stay in my old home town and serve Him with all of my heart right there. Still, I am hoping to return to visit both countries in the future, and I believe God will give me the opportunity to do just that.

As I write my closing lines, I now live in my hometown, St. Louis, MO. Many years later, I still miss my husband Patrick, and the wonderful life of joy God gave us together, but I have grown deeper in my love and compassion for others. I have matured spiritually and emotionally through all the challenges I faced and believe I am stronger and wiser for it. I can praise God now for my past, even my great loss as I know God had a plan in all of it. I can't see all of God's plan from this side of eternity, but one day I will see clearly.

I press forward, not looking back. One of my favorite scriptures is a guiding beacon for me: *"Not that I have already obtained all this or have already been made perfect, but I press on to take hold of that for which Christ Jesus took hold of me. Brothers, I do not consider myself yet to have taken hold of it. But one thing I do; forgetting what lies behind and straining toward what is ahead, I press on toward the goal to win the prize for which God has called me heavenward in Christ Jesus"* (Philippians 3:12-14).

I choose to live every day to the fullest – with God's joy and peace. It does not come easily; I must fight back lethargy, apathy and every lie of the devil daily. I conquer through worshipping my precious Redeemer and meditating on His Word every single day. I am going to live in victory. No, I might not always feel it, but I'm going to choose it today and the next and the next. Believe me,

I am no one special. I am just an ordinary lady who serves a very extraordinary God. I have always desired to be right in the center of what God is doing, and that usually involves taking a lot of risks. But along with the risks come overflowing joy, fulfillment, healing and peace. I surely wouldn't want to live any other way.

Thirty years ago God gave me a song of great hope and encouragement. I penned it and placed it as the title track on my first CD that I recorded two years after Pat's death. The song even won an honorable mention in a Nashville song contest out of thousands of songs many years ago. The name of the song and CD is *You Ain't Seen Nothing Yet*. I based it on my life scripture which I shared earlier in this book, *"Forget the former things, do not dwell on the past. See, I am doing a new thing! Now it springs up; do you not perceive it? I am making a way in the desert and streams in the wasteland."* (Isaiah 43:18-19.)

My life felt like that wasteland after Pat's death. But there was hope and a new life for me, and there is new life waiting for you too. You won't know what it is until you step out into the deep and just live it! Remember, you ain't seen nothing yet!

God said
Forget all what you've seen, forget all what I've done
O you ain't seen nothing yet
I'm doing a brand new thing in you; My plan is coming true
O you ain't seen nothing yet.
(Chorus of "You Ain't Seen Nothing Yet.")

Chapter 24

Lessons Learned from My Life and Loss

1. It's great to dream but realize life may not always work out like you think. God has plan B or C if plan A doesn't work out. *Jer. 29:11*

2. Keep your hope, even when all hope seems lost. *Ps. 27:14*

3. Don't stuff your emotions, but don't wear them on your sleeve either. Tell God and one good friend your problems. Talk and pray it out, but don't act them out! *Ps. 55 all*

4. Be real and authentic, but never rude. Don't worry about who likes you or who doesn't. There will always be someone who doesn't like you. Love them anyway. *1 Jn. 3:11-16*

5. Grief and sadness are a part of life and there is a process you must walk through in a loss, just don't stay there forever. God will heal you. Time doesn't heal, but GOD does. *Isa. 60:20*

6. Life is short. Have no regrets. You don't know what tomorrow holds so make the most of every single day. Enjoy the present and don't look back. You may not get a second chance. *Mt. 6:34*

7. People & friends will hurt and disappoint you. Make the choice to forgive them and keep on forgiving. Remember, you have hurt others too. *Lk. 11:4.*

8. Make God your very first priority, then your spouse and children. God will bless your life when you keep your balance with Him first. *Mt. 6:33*

9. Fear and dread will kill you. Study God's Word daily to live in peace, trust and rest. *2 Tim. 1:7*

10. Be thankful for what you do or did have instead of being miserable or complaining about what you don't have. Choose to live in contentment—no matter what. It's not your circumstances that make you feel the way you do, it's how *you handle* the circumstances. *Phil. 4:12*

11. Count every blessing everyday, even if it's just one. Don't count your problems, period. Leave them with God. *Ps. 34:1*

12. Don't isolate yourself. Go help someone else worse off than you. Make a phone call. Just get out of the house and volunteer somewhere. Just DO IT! *James 2:14-17*

13. Self pity and the "why me?" game will sap all your energy, strength and joy. Stop it in its tracks and start counting your blessings immediately. *I Cor. 10:10*

14. Pray, worship and thank God daily. Receive His love every day through prayer and His Word. You will stay strong and refreshed. *Col. 1:9-12*

15. You are what you say because you say what you think you are. Think Godly thoughts – it takes practice. Write down positive scriptures and memorize them. *Prov. 23:7*

16. Kindness, like love, never fails. Even when you think you can't be kind one more second, ask God for grace to love and be kind. He will give it to you quickly! Practice kindness; it gets easier. *Eph. 4:32*

17. Stress and worry is NOT God's plan for your life. Believe God and His Word instead. Meditate on God's Word and His peace until it becomes second nature. *Jn. 14:27*

18. Life isn't easy, in fact many times it is very hard. But God's love never will fail or leave you. He will walk with you and hold you tight through every trial. *Heb. 13:5-6*

19. Rejoice in the Lord always, again I say rejoice! *Phil. 4:4*

20. Choose to live life in victory daily knowing that all things work out for good for those that love and serve God – and you can go to the bank on that! *Rom. 8:28.*

If you've read this book, you've seen how God the Father, Son and Holy Spirit have radically redeemed and changed my life and that of my late husband, Patrick. We were never the same after that! This salvation that we found is for anyone who calls on His name for "anyone who calls on the name of the Lord will be saved." (Romans 10:13). This wonderful free gift of salvation and freedom in Jesus Christ is for *you*. Yes, *you* - right this very minute!

It is not something that can be earned. You can never be good enough to get to heaven, *"for we all have sinned and fallen short of the glory of God, every single one of us"*. (Romans 3:23). All of your deeds, church attendance or prayers alone can't earn your salvation.

Salvation- being forgiven of your sins and experiencing new life in Christ and life eternally with Christ in heaven, is only possible by what Jesus, the sinless Son of God did for you on the cross at Calvary. Jesus took on human nature and became like you, but without sin. He gave His life freely, even to be put to a gruesome and painful death so that you could live for all eternity with Him in heaven. That is His plan for you and *that* is how great His love is for you!

When you accept Jesus as the new King and ruler of your life, this is what happens- let me quote directly from the Bible: *"Since the children have flesh and blood, He too shared in their humanity so that by His death He might destroy him who holds the power of death—that is, the devil—and free those who all their lives were held in slavery by their fear of death. For surely it is not the angels He helps, but Abraham's descendants. For this reason He had to be made like His brother in every way, in order that He might become a merciful and faithful high priest in service to God, and that He might make atonement for the sins of the people. Because He Himself suffered when He was tempted, He is able to help those who are being tempted."* (*Hebrews 2:14-18.*)

Jesus took your place of eternal death and damnation that you deserved and actually became sin, your sin on the cross, and in its place offers you eternal life with Him! (2 Corinthians 5:21.)

Salvation is simple, not complicated. I didn't know even one scripture the night I cried out to God on my living room floor. I just asked Jesus, if He was real, to save me and forgive my sins. That was it. And He did—radically! I had tried being good, but that didn't work. I tried living on the wild side, but that was worse! Jesus was my last hope; there was nothing left for me. Jesus *was then* and *still is* the answer. He is always more than enough, even thirty years later.

If you want to know God, the Creator of the universe and His Son Jesus, ask Him now to take control of your life. Tell Him you are sorry for every one of your sins and ask Him to forgive you. Believe that Jesus is the Son of God who gave His life in place of yours on the cross, rose again from the dead and will now live in your heart if you only ask Him. *Be born anew, again* (John 3:3) of the Spirit *right this very moment.* Just ask Him—right now! It's that simple.

Welcome, dear friend into the kingdom of God! I'm rejoicing with you!

Sandy Whalen, woman of faith, was inspired years ago with God's compassion to reach God's hurting children all over the world; first to Calcutta, India and later to nine other countries. She has pioneered outreach programs for the homeless and disenfranchised for over 20 years, including Rochester, NY where she also ministered extensively in correctional facilities. Besides the outreach ministries in Rochester and now in St. Louis, she began and currently directs a support group for widowed and divorced ladies, 'Women of Restored Destinies.'

Sandy, a graduate of Elim Bible Institute, Lima, NY and ordained minister, is also a speaker, songwriter and musician. A proud grandmother, she resides in Arnold, MO with her poodle, Cuddles. For more information or a speaking engagement, contact her at: restoredwomen@yahoo.com or via Facebook: Sandra Huddle Whalen.

CPSIA information can be obtained at www.ICGtesting.com
Printed in the USA
BVOW02s1123220715

409222BV00004B/4/P